# Yesterday's Treasures

## Blueberry Beach Novels, Volume 1

Jessie Gussman

Published by Jessie Gussman, 2021.

This is a work of fiction. Similarities to real people, places, or events are entirely coincidental.

YESTERDAY'S TREASURES

**First edition. February 20, 2021.**

Copyright © 2021 Jessie Gussman.

Written by Jessie Gussman.

**Cover art by Julia Gussman[1]**
**Editing by Heather Hayden[2]**
**Narration by Jay Dyess[3]**

Click HERE[4] if you'd like to subscribe to my newsletter and find out why people say, "Jessie's is the only newsletter I open and read," and "You make my day brighter. Love, love, love reading your newsletters. I don't know where you find time to write books. You are so busy living life. A true blessing."

1. https://sweetlibertydesigns.com/services/

2. https://hhaydeneditor.com/

3. https://www.acx.com/narrator?p=A3VWKVSC6MFZHW

4. https://BookHip.com/FASFD

# Chapter 1

THIS IS THE LETTER that Adam Coates found sitting on his kitchen counter the day his wife left him:

*Dear Adam,*

*I'm sorry this is going to come as a shock to you. I've tried to figure out how to tell you, and I just haven't been able to.*

*I want you to know, first of all, that I admire your dedication to your job and the business that you've built, and that you get up every morning and you work hard.*

*But I guess what you don't see is it was a single-minded dedication, and you've neglected your family in order to be a success.*

*I know I should have said something sooner, and the fault is mostly mine, except you are never here.*

*I didn't feel like this was a conversation we should have through texts.*

*You don't know it, because you haven't been around, but I was laid off from my job six weeks ago.*

*Maybe you don't remember, but I used to talk to you all the time about how much time you spent at your job and how I felt alone and neglected.*

*We didn't fight. I just tried to talk to you, and you would tell me that I was being dramatic or that it was what you needed to do in order to be successful and didn't I want you to be successful?*

*So yes, of course I did. So when I asked you to go get ice cream with me and you told me to do it by myself, when I asked you if we could have a date night and you said you were too busy, when I asked you to mark on your calendar Sierra's field trip but you couldn't because you were already planning to go somewhere else for your business, when I asked if we could take a weekend away and you didn't have time...when you forgot my birthday, when our 20-year anniversary came and went and you never said a word, when you took me out the last time and spent the entire time we were in the restaurant on the phone with one of your business associates...I didn't say anything.*

*I guess I'm saying something now.*

*I'm moving into the beach house. I'm taking Sierra with me. I've already withdrawn her from school here in Pennsylvania and enrolled her at Blueberry Beach High.*

*I guess I would have told you I was doing that if you had been here.*

*I'm not angry, and I don't hate you, and I hope you don't hate me, but I'm tired of being alone. Tired of being a single mom. Tired of being married and washing your clothes and doing your shopping and cooking your meals and raising your child, and yet I don't have a friend or companion or someone to talk to or even someone to help me change a freaking lightbulb.*

*I'm not asking for a divorce. I'm just moving to our beach house, and I'll figure out what to do with my life there.*

*I would have talked to you about that too, if you had been here.*

*Of course, I understand if you don't want me and find another woman to neglect. I won't fight it.*

*I'd thank you for the twenty years together, but it's been more like fifteen years alone.*

*I wish you the very best.*

*Sincerely,*

*Your wife,*

*Lindy*

# Chapter 2

LINDY DROVE TOWARD their beach house outside of Blueberry Beach. Her daughter, Sierra, sat on the seat beside her. Sierra had headphones in, her cell phone in her hand, her thumbs running over it, and her feet propped on the dash.

A typical sixteen-year-old, and maybe a little bit belligerent because she had to leave the high school that she loved and start a new life somewhere else.

Just because her mother had decided to.

It had only taken eight hours to get here from their home just north of Pittsburgh, but she had to wait until Adam left for work at six o'clock before she could pull out.

After Adam left, she had to wake Sierra.

Adam hadn't even noticed that she'd packed her stuff.

He didn't come home until late, and he left early.

His business was doing fantastically well. They were making money and had been for years. Of course, when he'd just started, they'd had lean years. Everyone did.

When he first started out, she helped him with his books and took all the phone calls. Even with the baby crawling around, it wasn't hard. And Lindy loved it. Adam and she talked all the time about their plans and their dreams and their hopes for the business and family. It had finally gotten off the ground, and he moved to an office location where they had storage space as well as room for more employees.

She hadn't made the move with him because Lindy had been starting kindergarten, and it was only half a day. Someone had to be home in order to get her off the bus. Someone had to be home to put her on, since Adam left for work hours before the bus arrived.

She admired his hard work and his determination to succeed.

Still did.

It was a crowded market, but superior service would always draw customers, and Adam provided superior service.

He also provided well for them, once the business finally took off about five years ago. For a decade, they didn't draw much of a salary and barely had enough to pay the mortgage and buy groceries.

She'd always been able to squeeze out the light bill as well, but for a long time, they were a one-car family.

Lindy didn't mind, except that meant, of course, that she couldn't go to work with Adam since she had to wait to put Sierra on the bus. He didn't have time to run her back and forth, and he needed their one vehicle for his job anyway.

It was fine, except it was the beginning of the end.

She parked their car, a nice, almost-new SUV, in front of their cottage on the eastern shore of Lake Michigan and pressed the ignition off, keeping her hands on the wheel, staring at the house, and blowing out a breath.

This was the beginning of the rest of her life.

Beside her, Sierra's thumbs moved rapidly over her phone and Lindy wasn't even sure she'd noticed they'd arrived.

The house was boarded up for winter. The planters that she'd had sitting on each side of the walk had blown over. There was some debris in the yard, and one of the shutters hung crookedly down, held by a single screw.

The house looked neglected.

She felt like she could relate.

She didn't expect to be coddled in her marriage, but there wasn't really a point of having a marriage when she did everything alone.

This wasn't her walking out on her marriage, exactly. It was more like her giving up.

She'd tried to gently nudge Adam, to mention that she wanted to do more than just sleep together for six hours at night.

And the man worked hard. She had to give him that. She admired hard work.

But wasn't a married couple supposed to talk occasionally?

Weren't they supposed to do things together once in a while?

Weren't they supposed to have some kind of shared time somewhere?

She tried to quit questioning herself and focus on what she was going to do.

She and Sierra would settle in here, and she would see if there was a job or something she could get in the town of Blueberry Beach.

She had skills. She'd been managing a candy store for years since working her way up from starting behind the counter when Adam and she had bought a second vehicle.

Her job in Adam's company had long been taken over by someone else, and he didn't even suggest that she work with him.

One more thing she'd gone out and done by herself.

Managing a candy store couldn't be too much different than managing some other kind of store, and she wasn't afraid to start at the ground and build up.

To start with, all she needed was money for groceries and electricity since the property was paid for as well as her car.

For the last five years, Adam's business had done really well, and she didn't want for anything material.

She just wanted a husband.

Maybe it was natural to feel like since he never spent any time with her, never wanted to do anything with her, he didn't really want her.

That he didn't like her. And if she believed in falling in and out of love, she would say he'd fallen out of it.

But she was more of the mind that love was an action verb.

An action verb she'd tried to live out for the last fifteen years, despite the fact that she saw less and less of the man she was trying to live the verb out on.

How do you show love to someone who doesn't seem to want to have anything to do with you? How do you show love to someone you never see? How do you show love to a man who is never around?

She blew out one more breath, and although she knew she probably wouldn't be able to stop herself from looking behind occasionally, she really wanted to focus on keeping her eyes looking ahead.

She prayed for guidance. Although she definitely did not have a peace about this decision, she'd also had doors open in a miraculous way. At least getting Sierra taken out of school and put in Blueberry Beach High.

It just so happened that one of her friends had moved here not that long ago.

Coincidence?

Maybe Lindy was just trying to grasp at straws to get God's blessing on what she knew she shouldn't be doing.

She should stay with her husband no matter how alone she was.

But things worked out with Sierra, and although her daughter wasn't super thrilled about the move, she wasn't fighting her either.

Sierra's feet smacked to the floor as she cracked her gum and blew a bubble.

Lindy tapped her on the arm. "Take your earphones off for a minute."

Sierra straightened, slipped her feet into the flip-flops she wore despite the cool spring day, and tilted her head, pulling one piece of plastic away from her ear. "What?" she asked, not unkindly but in a tone that let Lindy know she was being annoying.

"I want you to help me carry our stuff in, and there will be some cleaning that we need to do."

"I have to go to school tomorrow. I want to spend the day relaxing."

"You can relax after the work is done."

"I'm glad you brought me along. That way you didn't lose your slave."

It was borderline rebellious, but Lindy let it go, because she had brought Sierra along when Sierra would have been much happier living in a single-parent home north of Pittsburgh rather than living in a single-parent home in Blueberry Beach, Michigan.

She got the keys out of the cup holder and opened her car door. The last thing she needed to do was lock her keys in the car on her first night in town.

She supposed that would be a way to meet people, but not the way she wanted to.

She'd be handling everything by herself.

Not that she hadn't handled the mundane as well as emergencies by herself for years, but there was always that peace of mind in the back of her head that Adam could help her if she needed it.

That peace of mind was gone.

It probably had been a fantasy most of the time she'd cherished it anyway.

She shoved her phone in her back pocket. It contained the code to her car, which she could use to unlock it in case she actually did lock the keys in the car or lose them, but she wanted to be extra careful.

Shoving her keys in her front pocket after tapping the button to open the trunk, she walked to the back.

Sierra started grabbing stuff immediately, but Lindy just stood and looked at it.

She hadn't brought any furniture. The beach house had its own. Not super fantastic stuff, but stuff that would do.

She'd never needed fancy.

And she certainly wasn't going to start now.

# Chapter 3

ADAM FINGERED THE LETTER. She must have left it yesterday morning. But he'd come home late and hadn't even gone into the kitchen, having picked up takeout on his way home.

He'd read it three times now.

Really, he should be on his way to work. He had an appointment with a client west of Pittsburgh just across the Ohio River in West Virginia, and he needed to be there in an hour.

If he didn't get moving, he was going be late.

He prided himself on never, ever being late.

His company had an immaculate reputation.

And maybe, now that it was as successful as it was, most business owners wouldn't still be out in the field doing installations themselves.

Adam prided himself on not being most business owners.

His business had actually been voted the number one small business in Pittsburgh last year. Which was saying something.

It was an honor, although he hadn't taken the time to go to the dinner and receive the award in person.

He put his heart and soul into the business, and he would make sure that it was successful. Except...he fingered the letter again.

Did she mean she was leaving for good?

What did she mean she would have talked to him?

They had just seen each other...had it really been two weeks ago? On Saturday morning, he was still home when she had gotten up to take Sierra to band practice. Or was it orchestra? Whatever the group of musicians were that had a clarinet in them. Or was it a flute?

She played something that she blew into.

Although Lindy had gone and bought it herself, he'd earned the money for it. And she'd bought a good one, at least he'd told her to.

That was years ago. Sierra was still playing it, wasn't she?

He looked around, realizing that while Lindy usually kept a clean kitchen, it seemed to be extra tidy.

And now that he thought about it, although their bedroom was still dark when he'd left... Was it even possible that he'd slept all night in their bed and didn't even notice she wasn't there?

Normally when he came in late, he didn't slide across the bed and snuggle up to her because he didn't want to wake her up.

It was out of consideration, not because he didn't like to sleep with his wife's body pressed to his.

That was one of the joys of being married.

Except he couldn't remember the last time they'd slept like that, because he always went to bed second and long after she did.

Now that he thought about it, he'd actually seen her last Sunday. They'd sat down in the kitchen together. She'd gone to church, and he'd been getting ready to run into the office to go over the spreadsheet he hadn't had time to review since he was out working in the field all week.

And he'd put that extra installation in, the emergency one with the rush order that he'd gotten paid twice as much as normal for, on Saturday.

She hadn't said anything about it. She'd barely said anything at all.

Of course, he'd had his mind on his work, and then he'd come home after dark.

But Lindy and Sierra hadn't been there.

Now he remembered. They'd been out getting ice cream, and when they'd come home, he'd been in front of the TV, catching up on the news.

Lindy had stuck her head in and waved at him.

He really hadn't looked away from the TV, but he'd waved back.

He took in a breath and blew it out slowly, setting the letter down on the counter and tapping his finger on it.

Maybe she had a point.

He took out his phone. He wasn't going to wonder about this. There was obviously a misunderstanding, and they could work it out.

**How long are you staying at the beach house?**

He waited, tapping his fingers on the letter again. Then checking the time. She would be up. She wasn't lazy. She'd done an excellent job of taking care of Sierra and their house and also working a job.

Speaking of. What about her job? Why hadn't she told him about her job?

**Permanently.**

He stared at that one word. *Permanently*.

**Maybe I don't want to move?** He hit send, puzzled with his brows drawn together. He didn't know what else to say.

**You don't have to.**

**So we're going to live separately? Don't you think this is something we should have talked about?**

Again, her letter had really answered that, he supposed. Why hadn't she talked to him?

But...she was right. He hated that she was right, because he hadn't even realized it.

**I tried to talk to you. You weren't very interested in listening.**

He hadn't realized things were this serious.

**I'm willing to talk now. I'm listening.**

**Do you really think this is something we should discuss over texts?**

No, she was probably right about that.

**Come home, and we'll talk. I'll stay home from the office on Saturday, and we'll talk in the morning.**

**Wow. I get the whole morning?**

Okay, so he could hear the sarcasm in that one. And Lindy wasn't typically a sarcastic person. She was fun and funny and sweet, and she would do anything he asked her to, and he loved spending time with her and always had fun when they did things together except...she was right. They hadn't done anything together for a really long time.

And she was right again. Because he hadn't asked her to do anything with him.

And she was right *again*, because she had asked him to do things with her, and he had told her to go ahead and do them but he didn't have time.

**You're right. I haven't spent much time with you lately. Let's fix that.**

**I don't think years of neglect is something that we can fix in a morning. I'm in Michigan. You go ahead and do what you've been doing. I know you're happy.**

But he had been working for her. Them. For their family. For Sierra.

**Then come back for more than a morning.**

**I have to leave. I'm taking Sierra to school.**

The letter had mentioned she enrolled their daughter in a new school. But it was this short, ordinary statement that made everything hit home. The statement that made him sink into a barstool, set his phone down on the counter, and put his head in his hands.

Everything she was saying was true. He hadn't meant to do any of it. He thought he was doing a good thing.

He picked up his phone.

**Can we fix this?**

The phone was dark and silent. Maybe she'd left already with Sierra, or maybe that was his answer.

He'd gone to church. They went to church together. Most of the time. Some of the time. Okay, he went on Christmas and Easter. Sometimes Easter.

He was proud of his family; he loved going places with them. They'd gone on vacation last summer. They'd spent two whole weeks at the beach house together.

He'd taken his phone and his computer, and he'd done some work...a little bit of work... So he caught up on a lot of paperwork that he'd been neglecting, because he was a control freak and didn't want to hand it over, and the stuff that he handed over he had to check and double-check, because it was his business and his responsibility to make sure it was done right.

But he'd walked on the beach with Lindy. Once. She'd seemed quiet, and he'd wondered about it at the time but...

He didn't have their pastor's phone number programmed into his phone, so he had to look it up online. He couldn't even remember the name of their church, and he figured it was pointless to try to text Lindy and ask.

Deciding that he'd stop at the church and grab the number on his way to the installation job in West Virginia, that's what he did.

He was working with a crew of three, and they were more than a little surprised when the boss showed up thirty minutes late.

He'd never fired anyone for being thirty minutes late, but he'd considered it, because being on time—being early—was a hallmark of his business.

He had trouble concentrating, and at 10:30, he told the guys to take a break.

He got his phone, walked to the corner of his client's yard, and placed the call to Pastor Rendell.

Thankfully, the man picked up on the second ring. "Hello?"

"Pastor Rendell. This is Adam Coates."

There was a silence on the other end as Adam tried to figure out how he could say what he needed to say.

Finally, the pastor said, "Who?"

"Adam Coates." Obviously, he wasn't in church as much as he thought he was. "Lindy's husband. I'm Sierra's dad."

"Oh. Adam. Yes. Lindy told me that she would be moving to Michigan."

"Did she mention she was moving without her husband?"

There was a brief pause and maybe an intake of air. "No. She didn't."

"Well, she did. She moved to our beach house in Michigan and took our daughter with her. She left me."

Saying the words aloud made them real. There was no one to see, so he just sank to the ground. Disbelief, shock, and, wow, a painful hole opened up in his chest. His stomach filled with putrid air and expanded, pushing up the back of his throat, making his ribs ache.

*His wife had left him.*

Lindy. Lindy to whom he'd been married for twenty years. The only woman he'd ever loved. The woman he had a child with; they had a business together and...

"Would you like to come talk to me? I had a few things I was planning to do today, but I can rearrange my schedule and meet you as soon as you want."

Pastor Rendell's voice sounded sympathetic but also businesslike, which was good. Adam didn't want pity or compassion, really. He wanted answers. One answer: how to get Lindy to come back home.

He had the installation job to finish, but suddenly, that wasn't nearly as important as figuring out what he needed to do in order to get his wife back.

"It'll take me an hour, hour and fifteen minutes to get there. Can we meet then?"

"Sure. You want to meet at the church? Or would you like to get lunch?"

Adam looked at the time. That would be close to lunchtime. He hadn't even thought about that. He wasn't hungry. Hadn't eaten anything all day but couldn't imagine putting something in his stomach. It felt too twisted. Painful. Ugly.

"I don't want to keep you from your lunch." But he wasn't sure that he wanted to talk about this in a restaurant. He wasn't even sure what there was to talk about. Maybe he shouldn't even be meeting with him.

Was there an answer? Lindy hadn't been very open to suggestions. She'd never texted him back.

"That's fine. We'll just meet here. You're not keeping me from anything."

"Okay," Adam said, and they hung up.

He sat there, his legs bent, his arms hanging off his knees, the phone in one hand, buzzing occasionally with text or message notifications, but he ignored it.

Like he'd ignored them all day.

His wife had left him. He couldn't even believe it.

Still, maybe there was a chance. Maybe there was something he could do. Maybe Pastor Rendell had the answers, and he could do something, anything, and she would come back.

He didn't know how long he sat there, thoughts churning through his mind. He was a problem solver. He fixed things. He built things. He worked with his hands, and he got things done.

But there was nothing to do, nothing to build. And everything to fix, but he didn't know how to start. There weren't any materials in front of him. There was just a wife who wasn't alongside him anymore. And he hadn't even realized it was going to happen.

She said she would have talked to him about it, but when?

Lindy didn't lie. She was honest and bright, and she always lived according to what was right. She wasn't afraid to do hard things.

She'd suffered through the ten years that it had taken in order to get their business off the ground and make it successful enough that they could actually afford to pay all their bills and buy a little extra.

He'd paid the properties off, and she had a nice car, and she had never complained, even when they didn't have anything. Once Sierra had been in school, she'd gotten a job, and she was the one who paid for all of their groceries and all of Sierra's clothes and school items, and well, to be honest he didn't even know what all she paid, because she did it. She kept the house books; he did the business.

He thought they were fine with that arrangement.

Done thinking about it, he stood up stiffly, walking around the house to where his crew stood in a circle, one of them puffing on a cigarette, one of them holding a bottle of soda.

"You guys are going to have to finish this job yourselves. I need to leave."

They all stood there staring at him. He'd never left a job before it was finished.

Finally, they nodded at him. One of them said, "That's fine. We've got it."

The one smoking the cigarette lifted that hand and waved it, a trail of smoke wafting around. "Don't worry about a thing, boss."

Adam wasn't really paying attention and nodded kind of absently as he thought about all the things he needed to say to Pastor Rendell.

Marshaling his arguments, so to speak. Trying to present a defense. And show that this was all Lindy's fault.

Because a wife wasn't supposed to just walk out on her husband. Obviously, she wasn't following the Bible. He was sure the pastor would be on his side, and he might even call Lindy and try to talk some sense into her.

Sure, the letter in his pocket was completely right, but he was right too.

He figured he'd gotten together a pretty good defense, and he might have even turned it into an offense by the time he pulled into the church parking lot.

In fairness, he felt like he should bring the letter so he could present both sides, so to speak. He wasn't trying to pretend that he was completely innocent.

What door did he go in? He sat looking at the church that he'd been to not as many times as what he'd thought over the years.

Finally, he decided to try a door on the side rather than going in the big doors at the back—or was it the front? Whatever doors took him into the sanctuary. He didn't think those were the right ones.

This was ridiculous. Normally, he didn't pitter-patter around about what door to go in. Normally, he was confident and assertive, and he got things done. He didn't sit and waffle.

Getting out of his work truck, he slammed the door, not bothering to lock it, since the church was in a rural area, and just strode with maybe not quite as much confidence as he usually had toward the side door.

Before he got there, the pastor had opened it and stuck his head out.

# Chapter 4

"YOU'RE RIGHT ON TIME. Come on in." Pastor Rendell held the door while Adam walked in. "Good to see you, Adam. It's been a while," the pastor said, holding his hand out, which Adam took and shook.

"Yeah. I know. I haven't been here as often as I should have been. But I do listen to preaching tapes and Christian radio."

Pastor Rendell nodded his head but didn't make a comment.

"We'll go to my office, right here." He walked up a few steps and opened the door to the office, walking in, then waiting for Adam to go through before he closed it behind him. "Nice weather we're having."

"Yeah. Warmer than I expected." He hadn't been thinking about the weather. Although he had noticed the daffodils and a few tulips blooming around the church.

It was that time of year, and Lindy's were probably blooming. But he hadn't even noticed their flowerbeds.

Pastor Rendell indicated one of the chairs in front of his desk, and he went around and sat on the other side. "You seem pretty preoccupied. We can just get started if you'd like."

"I am. I told you my wife left me."

"You did. Do you have any idea why?"

Maybe Pastor Rendell normally didn't open a counselling session so bluntly, but Adam didn't want to mess around with small talk. He opened his mouth—he was going to paraphrase her letter—but then he decided he could just let Pastor Rendell read it. So he did. Pulling it out of his pocket, he handed it to the pastor.

The pastor unfolded it and took his time while he read it.

Adam shifted in his seat, glad of the armrest, where he rested his forearms, but that was uncomfortable, so he shifted again, putting one foot down and setting an ankle on his knee.

He noted the books on the pastor's desk, held up with a book stop.

The calendar planner type thing.

A holder with some pens. The ever-present computer. Flatscreen, with the actual computer somewhere else. At least, Adam didn't see it.

Silence reigned in the office, not even broken by the ticking of any clock.

Adam fought the urge to squirm.

Finally, he was almost ready to interrupt when Pastor Rendell looked up. He waved the paper. "Is this all true?"

Was it?

He could hardly believe it was, but he had to say, "Yeah. It's all true."

"And you're questioning why she left you?"

Now Adam felt stupid. "I'm a business owner. If I don't run my business, we're not going to eat. I have to spend time running my business."

"How much time have you spent at home in the last week?"

"I was there each night to sleep."

"What time do you get home?"

"Eight or nine o'clock usually."

"And what time do you leave in the morning?"

"Six. Depends on what job I'm going to—sometimes earlier. This morning, I planned to leave at 5:30, but I left late, because of the letter."

"So she got up before you did this morning and left a letter on the table before walking out?"

"No. She left it last night or yesterday morning or yesterday sometime...sometime before she left yesterday."

"And you just saw it this morning?"

"That's right."

"And you didn't notice that your wife wasn't in bed with you last night? Do you guys share a room?"

It seemed like a probing question, but it was probably fair considering what he was here for.

"I don't like to wake her when I finally go to bed, so I stay on my side and try not to move too much." He felt stupid as he was saying that and kinda stumbled over some of the words.

"So that was a no. You didn't notice that your wife wasn't in bed with you last night?"

"That's right." He looked down at his hands. Then back up. "But I'm telling you, I didn't notice because I try to be considerate."

"If you come home late once and try not to wake her up when you get in bed, that's consideration. To come home late so often that that's how you normally get in bed, that's a problem."

"This can't be all my fault."

"Whoa." Pastor Rendell put a hand up. "Let's not talk about faults."

"But you need to call her and tell her to come back." He hated the desperation in his voice, but he couldn't keep it out.

The pastor leveled his eyes at him, and the room fell silent as the seconds crawled by.

The last words he'd said just kind of hung in the air, and thoughts swirled around him as the pastor just stared.

Finally, he said, "We can't talk fault. We can't talk blame. You can't change her. The only thing you can do is decide if you want to stay married and if you want to change yourself. And if you decide yes to those two questions, then you need to figure out what *you* need to do." Pastor Rendell shook his head. "It's up to you to determine what you can do to try to save your marriage. I can't do it for you. And you can't make Lindy do anything."

The pastor had spoken in a very logical and level tone.

Then he stopped and waited while Adam digested those words.

"But I don't think I deserve this."

"Life isn't about getting what we deserve. In fact, very seldom in life do we get what we deserve."

Adam couldn't argue with that. It was true. "So you're saying this is all up to me?"

"That's right. Up to you."

"That's not fair. What about her? What is she gonna do?"

The pastor lifted both hands up. He held his palms out and waved them back and forth. "Lindy is not in my office. You are."

Adam thought about that for a couple minutes. Lindy surely would want to try to work on their marriage. She'd want to save it. "But I know Lindy doesn't want to be divorced. That's what she says in her letter. She's not asking for a divorce. Obviously, she wants to save our marriage too."

"But she's not here. You are. Do *you* want to save your marriage?"

He was a worker. He fixed things. He built things. He was successful and respected, and he'd always just kind of assumed that his marriage would be there. Lindy wasn't the kind of woman who was just gonna leave him. Except...he *had* neglected her. And pretty badly.

"Do you think I can do it? It takes two people to be married."

"How long has Lindy been married by herself?"

Ouch. That was a question that hung in the air.

Adam's heart pounded. It hadn't occurred to him that this could be a permanent thing. Sure, she'd said she was living in Michigan permanently, but he didn't think that them being separated was permanent. When she said permanently, he didn't think she really meant permanently. They'd work it out, and she'd come back.

But the fact that she was gone, did that mean that she didn't want to work anything out?

"What do you think, pastor? What should I do?"

Pastor Rendell was a godly man, but he was also a very deliberate man.

He didn't answer the question immediately. He thought about it. And while Adam wanted an immediate answer, he appreciated a thoughtful response. He wanted the best response. He wanted the response that would work, that would somehow wave a magic wand over his marriage and bring his wife back.

"I think you're going to have to win your wife back. I think you're going to have a lot of work in front of you. I think you're going to need to commit to some major changes in your life." Pastor Rendell lifted his brows and scrunched his face up. "You're probably going to have to decide how badly you want this, because I think in order to save your marriage, you're going to have to lose some other things."

"Lose other things? Like what?" Adam threw up his hands. "If she wants my kidney, she's got it. I'll give it to her. My liver too. Or whatever she wants."

"Do you know what she wants?"

Adam moved his mouth. Of course he knew what his wife wanted. She was his wife.

But he closed it again. He hadn't even known she lost her job. He didn't know what she wanted to do from here. She hadn't talked to him about it. How long had it been since she'd talked to him about what she wanted to do?

Maybe she'd quit talking to him because he hadn't been listening.

"I guess she wants to live in Michigan at the beach house. In Blueberry Beach," he said kind of listlessly and maybe a little defeated.

"What do you think she wants out of you?"

Normally, he would have answered that question right away. He would have said she wanted him to provide for her, pay the bills, make sure she had a house to live in and a car to drive, and provide for their child, but he'd been doing all those things. And it hadn't been enough.

No. Not that it hadn't been enough. It hadn't been what she wanted.

"But we don't always get what we want," he said.

"I think if you want this to work, you're going to have to stop thinking about you. And think about her." As the pastor spoke, he reached over and took his Bible from the corner of the desk, opening it easily and finding the page he wanted quickly. "In the passage that talks about love in the Bible, first Corinthians thirteen, the great love passage, it talks about what love is. This would probably be a good chapter for you to memorize. I can read it to you, but I think you probably know it."

"I do. Charity suffers long and is kind."

"Right. But if you go on down, it talks about charity seeketh not her own." The pastor lifted his head, his finger still pointing to the passage he referenced. "I think a lot of times we're told love is a feeling. But in reality, love is an action. A lot of actions. And what you're doing, providing for your wife, paying the bills, giving her a place to live, taking care of your daughter monetarily, those are all actions. But you could have done that as a grocery store clerk, janitor, or an employee in someone else's business basically. But you want to have a successful business, and you've been working toward that." The pastor cleared his throat. "As I understand it, there were a lot of years when there wasn't too much extra, and your family pulled in and made do."

Adam's eyes didn't drop. "That's true. I can't make excuses for that, other than that's part of starting a business. Sometimes, it doesn't turn a profit right away."

"I'm not criticizing you for that. I'm saying your actions, of providing for your wife, are good. But that's just one small part of what a marriage is. A marriage has to be a lot more than just putting a roof over her head. Because much of what you've been doing with your business is not just about putting a roof over her head and providing for her, but there are definitely selfish motives there. Am I right?"

The pastor said that in such a way that Adam wasn't offended. He wasn't accusing Adam of anything, just asking.

The pastor was right. He could have provided for Lindy in a ton of other ways.

"You could have chosen to do something that would have left you with more time."

"I can't argue with that. I didn't spend enough time with her. That's true."

"When you love someone, you need to show it." The pastor held up a hand. "I know. You showed her you loved her by working for her." He put the hand down, then steepled his fingers on his desk. "I think sometimes we don't realize we need to show people we love them by doing things that say 'I love you' to *them*. And not just us."

Adam looked at him, trying to figure that out.

"If I give you a rock, you're gonna look at me and think I'm the nuttiest person in the world, and you're not really going to appreciate it. If I give an archaeologist a rock that has an artifact in it, that might show love." The pastor kind of chuckled. "Because I gave them something that was meaningful to them."

"I see. So she doesn't want me to take care of her?"

"I think you know better. But if all she does is wash your clothes, but she never dries them…you see how there is maybe not balance there?"

"Okay. I get it. You're saying that taking care of her wasn't enough." Adam didn't really want to hear that, because it wasn't an easy answer. It meant that everything he'd been working for had been the wrong thing.

"Right. And it sounds terrible, because you took care of her so well, but if that's all you do and you never spent time with her, what's the point in her being married? After all, if you weren't married and didn't have a child, she could take care of herself quite well, correct?"

"Yeah. She could."

"She might have even given something up, a job or education or opportunities, so that she could be with your child."

The pastor said that as kind of a question, and Adam nodded. When Sierra first went to kindergarten, Lindy had stayed home with her rather than go to work with him. He thought that was a good thing for her, but she ended up never being a part of the business again.

"Okay, pastor, I see. I've been taking care of her, but I haven't been spending time with her, and I've been neglecting her. So what do I do?"

He was tired of talking about the problem. He wanted to talk about solutions.

"Well, I already told you I don't think it's going to be easy. And I do think you're going to have to give things up."

"What's not going to be easy? And what do I have to give up?" He'd already said he'd give up a kidney; man, he'd give up anything to have his wife. How could she not know that?

"You said she moved out to Blueberry Beach, Michigan, permanently. That's what she told me too last Sunday when she said it was her last Sunday here."

"Yeah?"

Pastor Rendell leveled a look at him. Serious and focused. His voice was low. "If you want to be with your wife, you have to move to Blueberry Beach."

# Chapter 5

ADAM STARED AT THE pastor. Probably five seconds went by before he pulled himself together and got his mouth to work. "But I have a business to run. I can't just...leave."

The pastor sat there, looking at him, with his brows raised.

It took Adam a moment, maybe several moments, as he stared at the pastor, meeting his gaze, his brain chewing on the problem. "You mean give up the business?"

The pastor's brows lifted. He didn't say anything.

Adam almost opened his mouth to argue. He was going to argue. He was a working man. He couldn't just quit working.

Could someone run it for him?

And then a new thought occurred to him. What about their house?

They didn't need it, either. Not if she were going to be in Blueberry Beach permanently. If he gave up his business, he might as well sell the house too.

And he'd move to Blueberry Beach.

What would he do there?

"Okay. I need to give up the business."

Pastor Rendell separated his hands and kinda held them there, almost saying, "you decide."

"I might as well sell the house too."

Pastor Rendell did the same thing again. He didn't say anything.

"And I'll move to Blueberry Beach."

Pastor Rendell sighed. "It might not work. I can't guarantee if you do all of that, make that sacrifice, that it will be enough. In fact, I would say that's a really good start, but I'm almost sure that won't be enough."

"Selling my business and our house and moving to Blueberry Beach won't be enough? That's huge."

"But it wasn't the problem to begin with."

Adam thought about that. The business created the problem, but the problem was his wife had been alone. She'd felt neglected and unloved.

He couldn't believe she felt unloved.

All the things he'd done for her, but like Pastor Rendell said, she wouldn't even have been looking at those things.

If someone gave him a rock, he'd toss it aside. He didn't want a rock.

Lindy hadn't wanted a successful husband who was never around.

It hurt. But it was true. He got that.

"I'm not sure what I'll do when I get to Blueberry Beach."

"I don't know if I can help you. But if we just try to follow the principles outlined in God's word, I can give them to you. And you can try to put them in practice. God's word doesn't return void."

He'd heard that before and believed it, and part of his business was based on it.

Integrity and honesty and doing what he said. It was what he based his business on. And he'd thought he'd based his marriage on that too, because he certainly had never even thought about cheating.

He supposed there were other things he could do to sabotage his marriage rather than cheat.

It didn't take a rocket scientist to figure out that his wife didn't get married so she could sit alone in their home by herself doing everything by herself because her husband didn't make the time to do anything with her.

"Any parting words for me, pastor?" Adam asked.

Now that he had a path forward, he was eager to get started. He had a couple of ideas of where he could go and possibly sell his business. Some competitors who might be interested if he needed to piece it out.

He wanted to keep his guys working, but, he had to say, his marriage was more important.

He could get his house listed today too, if he got home in time. Maybe he could call a real estate agent on the way home.

"Just remember, what you give might not mean anything, unless it's something she wants. A lot of times in a situation like this, you're starting out with a negative balance."

"A negative balance?" His bank account definitely wasn't in the negative numbers.

"You're trying to make up for years of neglect. In an ideal world, she would cancel out that debt, and you could both start again fresh. That might not happen. You might have to work at chipping away at the debt before you can start putting deposits in and actually getting credit."

"You're talking numbers I understand. I get that." He could see that he needed to probably win her trust back, possibly her love.

He wasn't exactly sure how to do that, but they'd dated before they'd gotten married. He could figure it out. He'd won her once; surely, he could do it again.

"Thank you, pastor. I'm not going to take up any more of your time. I'm sure you're probably hungry," Adam said as he stood up.

Pastor Rendell stood up too and came out from behind the desk. "Most men in your position wouldn't have come to me. They would have either gone out and demanded their wife come back and not cared about the reasons, or else maybe they would have just let her go and found someone else to try to take her place."

"Someone else I could neglect," Adam muttered.

"Don't be too hard on yourself, but it's good that you're taking responsibility. Take more responsibility than what you're expected to take. Do more than what you're expected to do."

Adam nodded. Those were the kind of employees he wanted. Employees that did more.

"I'm trying to give you credit for what you're doing. It's more than most men I know would do. I think you truly love your wife. And I think you truly didn't realize that she was ready to walk out. And I think you want her back and your marriage back. And I think...I could be wrong, but I think you're actually going to do the hard things that it is going to take."

"She's worth it. Our marriage is worth it. I made vows, and I intend to keep them. And I know Lindy will too. She said she didn't want to divorce. That tells me it's not another man or anything like that. It's just exactly what she said. She was tired of being alone."

And maybe felt unloved, uncared for, and unappreciated. He wasn't stupid. He knew women needed different things than men did. And he hadn't been doing those different things.

He felt bad. Worse than bad. He'd been thinking all this time he'd been doing a good thing. But it hadn't been a good thing. And while his inclination was to get angry, he understood. And he could—would—take responsibility for it.

"What do I owe you, pastor?"

"You don't owe me anything. This is part of my job." Pastor Rendell slapped him on the back, and they shook hands. "Maybe you can let me know how it goes."

"Can I call you if I need you?"

"Of course. Anytime. Calls come to my cell phone, and I answer whether I'm home or here."

"Thank you. I guess you're on call all the time like I am. Doesn't your wife feel neglected?"

Maybe Adam shouldn't have asked that. In a normal situation, he wouldn't have, but he just poured out more about his personal life to Pastor Rendell than anyone else in the world knew. Even his wife. Which was sort of his problem.

"You know what? I struggle with that too. Because when people need me, like you did today, they want me to be here for them, and I feel like that's my job. I can hardly counsel other people if my marriage isn't doing well."

"Thank you. I was so desperate for some advice, for some encouragement, because all I could see was black."

"Well, hopefully you have a little bit of light at the end of your tunnel now, and it'll guide you in the direction that you should go. You're probably not going to do everything perfectly right off the bat. Hopefully, Lindy doesn't expect that."

"She's not unreasonable. I think I'll be okay. I'll let you know how it goes."

"Thanks. You do that."

Adam didn't quite feel like whistling as he walked out the door, because all of this was his fault. He had hurt his wife, and he hadn't even realized it. He'd been hurting her for a while and hadn't known.

But he wasn't afraid of hard work, and now he felt like he was armed with what he needed to know in order to get her back.

# Chapter 6

LINDY SAT ON THE FRONT porch step of the beach house, sipping a cup of tea.

The sun had set over Lake Michigan, and she'd watched it from her front porch. Relaxing.

She was sore and tired and not nearly as happy as she wanted to be.

She'd spent the last two days cleaning the house and getting it livable.

Sierra was in at the table doing homework, having been ahead in Spanish class but behind in math. She was frantically trying to catch up.

Lindy appreciated that she'd learned a good work ethic from her father.

Adam wasn't all bad.

Regardless, as dusk settled down, and the brilliant oranges of just a few minutes ago settled into dark night tones, and she pulled her sweatshirt a little tighter around her, she wasn't nearly as at peace as what she should have been.

Tomorrow, she'd go into town after Sierra went to school and see if there might be any jobs.

She had enough in her savings account that she shouldn't have to work for a while.

She'd gotten a little bit of severance pay when the candy store had closed, which made her more blessed than the other employees who had gotten nothing.

Their health insurance had always been independently purchased and paid for because of Adam being self-employed. She wasn't worried about that.

She'd see what she could do tomorrow when she went into town.

She did have a plan. If there wasn't any work in town, she was going to try freelance work online.

She could do that, or there were plenty of blueberry farms around; surely they would be hiring for something. She was young enough she could do some kind of manual labor, and she wasn't afraid to work. If they could live on that during the summer, they could live on her savings for a winter or two.

It wasn't ideal, but it could be done until she could figure something else out, maybe go to school and brush up on her administrative assistant skills.

Or possibly, she could go and become a nurse. South of Blueberry Beach was a new hospital. Even if she wasn't a nurse, she could get some kind of job there. Maybe as an administrative assistant or in food prep. She was interested in nutrition. She could make it a career.

Something would open up. She was sure of it.

Not that she'd really prayed about it, because she didn't think that the Lord was really going to help her leave her husband successfully.

And that was a bit of a problem, because she wasn't sure she could do anything successfully without the Lord's help. Although he did send rain on the just and the unjust equally.

She took a deep breath of the cold night air, fresh and clear and clean. Maybe it was her imagination, but it just filled her lungs with more and better oxygen than the air back home in Pennsylvania.

She'd have to talk to her parents soon. Let them know what she had done.

"Mom?"

She turned to see Sierra standing at the door. "Yes?"

"Can you come in here and help me with this problem?"

She stood immediately. Math wasn't exactly her best subject, but so far, she'd been able to recall what she'd learned in high school to help whenever Sierra had gotten stuck.

Her phone buzzed with a text before she'd made it up the step. She pulled it out of her pocket.

**Are you doing okay?**

Adam.

She supposed it was kind of him to think of her. Although it was weird, since he hadn't seemed to think of her at all when she was living in the same house as he.

**Yes,** she texted back simply. She didn't want to fight, and she didn't want to cast blame. She just wanted...she didn't even know.

**Good night.**

She didn't answer that one.

With one last look at the dark emptiness that she knew was Lake Michigan, she turned and walked into her house.

# Chapter 7

LINDY FINGERED HER purse as she walked down the sidewalk of the main street in Blueberry Beach. She could walk up the beach from their cottage to town. It was only about a mile. An easy walk.

But she had a list of things she needed to get at the hardware store, and she didn't want to have to carry them all back. Plus, she didn't exactly dress nicely, but she didn't want to be too ragged and windborne if she happened to have a spur-of-the-moment interview for a job.

Of course, finding a job in town the first time she tried probably wasn't going to happen, but she wanted to be prepared.

There was a diner, whose sign blinked OPEN, and it looked like several patrons sat inside.

It gave off cozy and cute vibes, and its name, The Blueberry Café, suited the town.

In fact, a lot of the shop names had "blueberry" in them.

Like the Blueberry Surf's Up shop across the street from the diner.

There was also Blueberry Beach Crafts.

And the hardware store which was simply Blueberry Beach Hardware Store.

It was at the far upper end, and she would go there last when she was ready to go home and pick up her things.

The shop fronts were cute, and most of them were open.

Traffic was light. She supposed most of the shops did the majority of their business in the summer months.

The candy store she'd worked in back in PA had depended on Christmas, Valentine's Day, and Easter to get them through the year.

Sales were light most of the rest of the time, and they really pushed things on the holidays.

She had tried to talk the owner into adding an ice-cream counter, a cool 1950s-style bar top with red vinyl barstools and chrome and complete with music even, which would have been really neat and probably a popular hangout for the teens in their area. That would have brought business in all summer long.

But it'd closed, and her idea had never been utilized.

There was one shop whose windows were bare, and there was a sign "For Lease" hanging in the window.

She stopped and stared at it. She couldn't tell what it had been before, but she could imagine a candy store.

It would take most of her savings probably. She could run some numbers, although she'd need to know how much the lease was first.

On a whim, she pulled her phone out and typed the number in, thinking at the very least she could call and find that out.

She got the number typed in as a man came up the street. She figured she'd wait until he went by before she started her call.

"Howdy. Beautiful morning," the man said.

"It sure is," she said, meaning it. She felt free, if not exactly happy.

There was a deep sadness that made her bones ache, a feeling like she'd left part of herself behind. But there was also the idea—an exciting idea—that she could do something new, start over. Be somewhere where people appreciated her, maybe.

"You thinking about leasing that?" the man said.

He was a complete stranger, and she wasn't in the habit of having personal conversations with men and especially not complete strangers. Still, what else could she say since he'd seen her typing the number in her phone?

"I'd considered it. Do you live around here?" She figured she could ask a personal question of her own.

The man held a hand out. "Name's Gage. And yeah, my two daughters and I actually live above the shop you're looking at right now."

"I'm Lindy. And that's nice. How long have you lived there?" she asked as she shook his hand—a firm grip but soft hands. The man must work at a desk for a living.

"A few years now. I rented it after my wife walked, thinking I'd eventually get something nicer, but the girls actually really love living right here on the beach, and it was an ice-cream parlor and treat store until last fall, and my girls worked the counters. It was convenient to have them right there. And they loved making extra money. Anyway, I guess I'm saying I could have moved, but I didn't want to." He put a hand through his hair. "Still don't, really."

She nodded. Although she liked the privacy of their summer cottage, she could understand the appeal of living right in town yet so close to the beach.

"In the summer sometimes, it gets a little crowded, but the rest of the year, it's fabulous here. We don't really have a yard or anything, but we've got the whole beach. What more could a man ask for?"

She nodded. "It's gorgeous. Nice for you."

"That's right. Great place to exercise every morning. And the sunsets are gorgeous."

"Sounds great."

They stood there for a moment in awkward silence, and he shuffled his feet a little bit.

Finally, she said, "How old are your daughters?"

"Fifteen and seventeen. A freshman and a junior. Can't believe they've grown up so fast."

"Oh. My daughter's sixteen. She's a junior as well. She probably knows yours."

"I'll have to ask. What's her name?"

"Sierra. And yours?"

"Naomi is seventeen, and Lexi is fifteen."

"And you said this was an ice-cream parlor?"

"It was. Pretty. And popular too. I don't think the proprietor left because of any financial difficulties. But her parents, who retired in Florida, needed someone to care for them. So she went down south."

"I see."

"Well, I'm going to head over there to the diner. The lady who runs it, Anitra, has a son who's having some health issues." He lowered his voice. "Cancer. As I understand it, he was given a couple of months. If that."

"Oh, that's terrible."

"Yeah. So we've all been kind of pitching in to try to keep the diner open."

"We?"

"All business owners up and down the street. I'm not a business owner here, but I run my business online, and with my phone, and yeah, everybody on the street is giving her a hand. However long it takes, she can't be without income."

"I see. Well, I was going to head over there and grab a bite to eat. It's open. The sign's blinking."

"Yeah. That's what I was saying. We're all pitching in."

"I'll be over."

"If you walk over now, I'll walk with you."

"I'm married." She hated to tell him no. She didn't want to seem rude, especially since it seemed like everyone who owned a business on the street were part of one big, happy family, but she also wasn't free to just walk to lunch with the man. "My husband's in Pennsylvania." Totally arbitrary information, but she just wanted to be clear. "I think I'll give this number a call before I come over."

"Suit yourself. I'll see you in a bit." Gage waved as he looked both ways then walked across the empty street.

Lindy didn't want to go. He was probably about her age, and she supposed he was good-looking. Not that it mattered to her. He seemed nice and friendly, and there was an openness about him that made her feel like he didn't have an agenda and wasn't trying anything.

His expression hadn't changed when she mentioned her husband, and she felt like his offer to walk her to the diner was made just because she had said that that was where she was going. It eased her mind a little, and she pushed him from her thoughts.

Pressing the button, she held her phone to her ear, thinking she would just ask the price.

The phone rang so long she wasn't sure anyone was going to pick up, but finally, after what must have been ten rings, a voice on the other end said, "Hello?"

"Hello." She cleared her throat, thinking she should have done that before she started the call. "I'm Lindy Coates. I am..." It had been so long since she'd made a call to anyone other than her friends and occasionally a customer service representative. She could do it. "I'm calling about the property that is available for lease on Main Street in Blueberry Beach."

"Okay."

Then silence on the line.

Lindy's fingers tightened on the phone. "I might be interested in putting in a candy shop. But in order to...complete my business plan, I need to know how much the monthly lease is and what it includes."

It took her a bit, but she finally got warmed up, and she was doing okay by the end of that sentence.

The call lasted about five minutes while the person informed her that someone else had already called about it, and while they gave her the numbers and information she'd asked for, along with some she hadn't, they told her that they couldn't guarantee it would be available.

After giving her number and asking to be informed if the first person in line didn't come through, she ended the call.

It had looked like a perfect opportunity, but maybe it wasn't.

The sun was high in the sky, and the day had warmed up to a pleasant temperature, even with the breeze that blew in from the lake. She loved that fresh breeze and the way it lifted her hair and just kind of lifted her spirits with it.

With a renewed spirit of optimism, she took a deep breath and blew it out with her face to the wind.

Crossing the street, she walked into the diner.

It was cute, with a bell that jingled above the door and a counter with the board above it listing mostly breakfast dishes.

She'd noticed on the door that it was open from five until three.

She could imagine people who jogged in the morning probably took their jog and then popped into the diner for a coffee. She saw a lot of cappuccinos and other coffees listed on the far left part of the board. Maybe they'd get an iced coffee in the summer.

There were surfboards hanging on the wall, along with seashells and other beach décor. The place looked fun and beachy while still feeling cozy. She liked it.

Ordering a turkey sub with tomato and onion, she paid and then picked out a seat.

She sat, looking around at the few other patrons in the store and the occasional car that went up and down the street. The beach wasn't super busy, but there were people, not swimming but who seemed to come for exercise or maybe just to enjoy the view.

It didn't feel like very long at all when Gage brought her food out.

"I think I've seen you before."

"You have. Thank you," she said as he set her food down.

"How'd your phone call go?"

"There is someone else already interested. They'll call me back if it's available."

"I guess that's the best you can hope for. If it's meant to be, it'll be."

"It sure will." She really hoped it was meant to be. "Did you cook this?" she asked, looking at the gooey melted cheese sliding down the turkey on her sandwich. Her stomach rumbled.

"I did. I had a little crash course in food prep a couple days ago. It's not too bad. We're not typically too busy after the breakfast rush, which gets kinda crazy. Dr. Chambers cooks breakfast which mostly consists of omelets. He does a pretty fine job."

"I'll have to come and try them."

"You should. Enjoy your sandwich. And if you have any pointers, I'm all ears."

"I'll remember that."

He smiled and waved as he left. This time, she didn't want to walk away.

But seeing Gage again made her think about Adam.

Adam was maybe not quite as tall. He had more hair. He was much more serious. Driven. Not that he didn't love to joke, because he did, and they used to have a lot of fun together. But Adam probably wouldn't take the time to talk to a random woman on the street, and he definitely wouldn't remember that she was making a phone call and think to ask her about it.

At least not the Adam of modern times. Maybe Adam back in the Stone Age, when they dated and were first married. He might have back then.

Still, Gage just didn't look right. He didn't act right. Didn't have the right tone of voice. He just wasn't...wasn't Adam.

She picked up her pickle and took a bite of it.

She had promised herself she wasn't going to think about her husband. If he'd wanted her, he would have spent time with her. He wouldn't have completely ignored her for months. Years.

She didn't linger, and she didn't say more than thank you to Gage when he came out to bring more food to new patrons.

She threw her garbage away, stacked her plate with the rest of the dirty dishes on the spot on top of the garbage can, and walked out, wondering if maybe she wasn't meant to work in Blueberry Beach.

There were no help-wanted signs.

It looked like the diner in town was struggling, and everyone was working to help with that.

Picking up the list of items that she needed at the hardware store, she decided she'd give herself another day or two. Maybe the person leasing the store would call back.

In the meantime, there were a lot of repairs she needed to make on the beach house. She might as well get started.

She'd not quite made it to the hardware store when her phone rang with the number she recognized as the one she'd just called.

Fifteen minutes later, she'd set up a time to sign a lease, and she never had finished that business plan. Still, she couldn't help but feel that everything was going to work out.

# Chapter 8

LINDY HELD HER PAINTBRUSH up and looked at the sign. Blueberry Candy Cream. Sierra had actually come up with the name of the store.

The rent had been within her budget, although swinging it would be hard. And she almost certainly would have to come up with some additional work in the winter.

Regardless, in their second conversation, she'd been given the phone number of the previous owner and had been able to make all the vendor contacts that she needed.

She'd applied for licenses and permits, and now, six weeks later, she was almost ready to open.

She'd done a lot of the interior work herself, having had to hire out for some, including putting some shelving in and a cooler.

She also bought some patio tables for outside her shop, to set on the sidewalk. Just a couple, but it lent a nice atmosphere.

All of that meant she hadn't been able to get the work on the beach house finished.

But she had plans, once the store opened, to work on the beach house in the mornings before she went in to the store.

Unless she helped Anitra, the owner of the diner whose son was struggling with cancer.

She picked her phone up and stepped back, far enough that she was able to get the entire sign in the picture. It was a cute cotton candy blue and pink with some highlights in yellow and purple. A fun, beachy type sign that she hoped would make people smile.

She wasn't trying to go for the serious professional look.

That wasn't what Blueberry Beach was about, and it wasn't her either.

As she picked up her phone, a text came up on the screen immediately, and she looked at it.

**Are you doing okay?**

It was what Adam texted every night since the second night she'd been in Blueberry Beach.

Every night, she texted back, **I'm fine.**

She figured eventually he'd probably stop. She was surprised he'd been doing it this long. It was more attention than he'd given her for months, years, when she lived with him.

He hadn't talked about getting back together, and she had to admit part of her was disappointed.

Maybe a little part of her thought that her moving out would wake him up. She should have known better. Making his business work meant everything to him. There wasn't anything that was going to stand in his way. He had huge plans for it and intended to grow it big.

And honestly, she hoped they all came true. She didn't begrudge him any success. As hard as he worked, he deserved it.

He just wasn't going to have success *and* a wife. He had chosen one and neglected the other.

She turned away from the sign, putting the lid back on the paint can and pounding it down with the handle of her brush.

She couldn't think about Adam, because she'd eventually feel guilty, like she should have continued to stay, even though he didn't even notice she was there.

The guilt came mostly because she was robbing her daughter of a father. Maybe she should have waited until Sierra graduated. She'd made it sixteen years, what was another two?

She painted the other side of the sign yesterday, and once this side dried, Gage had told her that he'd help her hang it. He would need to come out to their house and take their ladders in, since she didn't have a pickup.

The beach house had a shed which contained a hodgepodge of tools and, thankfully, two ladders.

Opening day was scheduled three days from today. Saturday.

After talking to Gage and several of the other business owners whom she had gotten to know by eating at the diner, not every day, but at least getting a coffee and being social, they suggested Saturday as the best day to open since it was typically the busiest day.

She figured they had businesses here, so they would know, and she was taking their advice.

She set the paint aside, thinking to take it down to the shed, and dropped her brush in the can of water she kept there for that purpose.

There was time to take a little walk on the beach before she took a shower and before Sierra came home. She was sitting down to take her sneakers off when a car pulled over the little rise and came up the driveway.

A pickup, actually. It wasn't Gage's pickup, since his was a dark color and this one was white.

It looked kind of beat up and was not one she recognized. Not from in town, and it definitely wasn't Adam, despite the jump in her heart rate.

She hadn't even realized she was hoping he would come after her. Still. After being gone for six weeks.

To her surprise, she was disappointed as soon as she realized it wasn't Adam's pickup. Had she really thought he would take time off to come talk to her?

He would call her on the phone first. She was sure of it. Adam wasn't going to waste time driving out here if there wasn't any use in coming.

And she would disabuse him of any notion that he needed to come as soon as she spoke with him. She wasn't going back.

What was the point?

If she were going to live by herself, she might as well live by herself somewhere she wanted to live, instead of living in a house that was supposed to be a home for a family but instead was where she spent her days as a single mother.

The pickup pulled into the parking area, wide enough for two vehicles, and parked beside her car.

The person behind the wheel had a ball cap on, and she couldn't really see his face, but...he seemed to be staring at her.

Their beach house was kind of secluded. It sat at the front middle of the twenty acres they owned.

She wasn't exactly sure where the line to their property was and where the line to the beach started. Somewhere around the sand dunes, but that didn't matter right now.

A slither of apprehension went through her. She was here alone.

Sierra was practicing with Naomi and Lexi and the other kids in the summer beach band.

Just a bunch of kids and some adults who got together and played music on the beach during the summer with a hat in front of them, or an open instrument case, and they split the tips they got.

Currently, some of those adults were donating their time to help the youngsters, although it was all self-motivated.

Sierra was very motivated. She hadn't exactly settled in Blueberry Beach like a duck to water, but there were a lot of things she enjoyed, and hanging out with Naomi and Lexi was one. Lindy fully intended to use all three girls at the counter of the candy shop when it opened.

Sierra's passion for playing the clarinet and making music with her friends was another thing she enjoyed.

They didn't have this back in Pennsylvania.

The man in the pickup was still staring at her, and she was tempted to back up, getting ready to run into the house, although it wasn't like the door to the beach house was super sturdy. The windows were open, letting in the fresh, warm spring air.

He could get in if he wanted to. Unless she was very, very quick.

But then the driver's door opened, and the man got out.

Lindy narrowed her eyes. As soon as he shut the door, she knew who it was.

Adam had come.

# Chapter 9

ADAM STOOD BESIDE HIS pickup, staring at his wife.

She looked a lot different. Her hair had been bleached to a soft golden blonde, and her skin had been darkened by the sun, like she'd been spending a lot of time outside. She had some kind of material tied around her hair, knotted at the top and kind of flopping on the sides, casual and a little flirty.

It was probably meant to keep the hair out of her eyes, but she had apparently been working long enough that it blew around her face in wispy strands.

She was slimmer than he remembered. Her fitted T-shirt curved in at the waist and flared out a little at the hips.

Her jeans were loose and had what looked like splatters of paint on them. She wore flip-flops and no smile.

Very much not like Lindy.

She stared at him, hand over her eyes, blocking the sun, as he stood there. He supposed he should say something.

Maybe he should walk toward her.

His heart pounded in his chest, and his stomach had a death-grip hold on his backbone.

She looked good. Better than she had when she was living with him.

He supposed he looked worse. He hadn't had a haircut since she left, but it didn't really matter, since it was thinning on the top anyway.

He wore a ball cap, so she wouldn't know that right away. Although probably there were tuffs sticking out along the sides of his hat. He didn't know. He had dressed a little nicer, thinking that he might see her when he got here, and he wore a button-down tucked into jeans that were fairly new.

He wore cowboy boots rather than his work boots, because Lindy always liked them.

His shirt was green, because she always said that brought out the depths of green in his eyes.

Plus, green was her favorite color.

Little things. Little things he hadn't thought about for a long time but that he'd done for her.

Sometimes, Lindy noticed things like that.

Most of the time, he didn't.

He swallowed hard, which didn't make his throat feel any better, but it kept him from drooling.

He took a few steps forward, walking around the truck and stopping at the walk, five feet from his wife. The wife he hadn't seen in almost six weeks.

"Hey there," he said, wishing he had some kind of great, wonderful words to say that could tell her everything he felt and would win her back immediately.

He didn't have any words like that, and he guessed that Pastor Rendell was probably right.

He had talked to Pastor Rendell three or four more times. The last time was yesterday.

Pastor Rendell had put together a little booklet for him, of advice and suggestions.

Some Bible verses too.

He hoped it worked.

There was only one thing in the world that he wanted.

Only one thing that mattered.

She was standing in front of him now.

"Hey," she said, and while it sounded friendly, it sounded like the kind of friendly she might say to a stranger. Not the kind of friendly she might say to her husband whom she hadn't seen in six weeks and was really happy to see again.

"I sold the house."

Her eyes flickered, but then her shoulder lifted.

He had bought it before they were married; it was only in his name. He hadn't needed her to sign. Or she would have known.

"That's nice," she said in the same tone she might have said "we got a lot of rain last night."

"I sold the business."

This time, there was more than a flicker in her eyes. Her brows went up, and her lids fluttered. Then her eyes narrowed. "Really?"

He nodded. "Really."

"You sold it?"

"Yeah."

"You didn't keep any of it?"

He shook his head no.

"Where are you working?" she asked, her brows pinched in, and he had the feeling she was asking in spite of herself. Like she didn't want him to know she wanted to know something about him. Maybe she didn't. Maybe she was just asking because she couldn't believe it.

Maybe she really didn't care.

He held his hands out in a "here I am" kind of way. "I'm unemployed."

"You don't have a job?"

He shook his head.

"Did you apply for one somewhere?"

"Not yet."

"Oh. So you're going to."

"I don't know. I guess it depends on you."

That made her brows shoot up again. "On me?"

Some kind of bird, he wasn't sure what it was, tweeted a song, and he wondered something he had never wondered before. Was it a male bird singing for his mate? Asking her to reconsider taking him back?

"How does it depend on me?" she asked, like she truly didn't know.

He didn't want to say. Because everything depended on her. He'd sold everything, given everything up, left his home, left his parents—who weren't very happy about it—and followed her to Blueberry Beach.

He supposed he was silent long enough, trying to figure out what to say, that she'd given up on him answering.

"What are you going to do?" Now her eyes were narrow, almost as though she was getting ready to tell him that he wasn't living with her.

"I'm moving to Blueberry Beach. And I'm going to work here as long as you're here. Somewhere."

"Here?" she asked, with an odd note in her voice.

He nodded. "In Blueberry Beach."

"You're moving here?" An expression that he might describe as horrified seemed to take over her face. "To the beach house?"

He hadn't figured she would want him to move in, but her expression hurt just the same.

How had he allowed his marriage to get to this point? He hadn't even known.

He wanted to ask her a million questions. Starting out with "why didn't you grab a hold of me and tell me that you were going to go if I didn't straighten up?"

He wasn't sure that would have changed things.

If it had, it probably wouldn't have been for long. He might have been "okay, fine, let's schedule a night to go out." And that would have been it.

He thought maybe that wouldn't have been enough. It would have just delayed the inevitable.

He shoved a hand in his pocket. "No. I wasn't going to move into the house."

She lowered her head slightly and lifted her brows, and he read the expression easily.

She wanted to know where, exactly, he was going to live.

"We have twenty acres. Is it okay if I find a spot somewhere?"

She just stood there, her arms crossed over her chest, staring at him, trying to figure out what he was saying. Confusion was stamped on her face, along with annoyance.

Almost as though she didn't like him stepping out of the lines of what she thought he was going to do and doing something different, because it was messing up her plans.

He definitely didn't want to mess up her plans, but he did want to be a part of them. If he could.

"What are you doing?" she finally asked.

He flexed his jaw. This is what he had been debating the entire way here. Should he be open with her about what he wanted? Or should he just do what he planned and hope his actions spoke for themselves and that she would fall for him again?

If he told her, he ran the risk of her deciding that she wouldn't let him win, no matter what he did. That she was set in her ways.

But Lindy had never been stubborn. She had never been determined to get what she wanted. She'd always been easygoing and ready to roll with whatever came their way.

That, coupled with the fact that he didn't want to be underhanded, that he wasn't trying to do anything wrong, in fact, he was trying to do things to right a wrong...every time the thought had wrestled in his head, he had decided that he needed to be forthright with her. As much as she was willing to listen to him.

He began, humbleness in his tone. "When you left, I didn't get a chance to give my opinion about what I wanted."

"You didn't get a chance? Because you weren't home. Ever." There was definitely irritation in her voice now.

He probably deserved it.

"All right. Because I wasn't home, I wasn't able to give my opinion about what you and Sierra were doing. And after about five minutes of standing in our kitchen, holding your note, I decided if you wanted to live in Blueberry Beach, that's where I would be too."

"Five minutes? I'm sure it took you longer than that to decide you had to sell your business and our house. If you really did." She added that last on, but she knew he was honest. It was something he prided himself on. He had faults. Lots and lots of faults. But dishonesty wasn't one of them.

It was his turn to lift his brows.

"All right. So you decided you want to live in Blueberry Beach. I believe you." Her posture said that she didn't care. She stuck her jaw out with her eyes narrowed. A mulish expression he'd barely seen in their two decades together.

"Because, as I read your letter, I realized that...you're right. You were right about everything. That wasn't where I wanted to be. You are too valuable to lose."

She pulled both her lips in and bit them, which was something she always did when she tried not to cry.

The sun must be setting behind him. He couldn't see it, but there was an orange glow on her face. Her eyes were in shadow, and there wasn't quite enough light for him to see if she was tearing up. Not that he wanted her to. He just wanted to be honest.

"I realized that everything that I was working for wouldn't be worth anything if you aren't with me." He held a hand up, and she took a breath and opened her mouth. "I know. That's not the way I was acting. I acted like it didn't matter if you were there. And...I was being selfish."

"Don't think that you can come here, and say the words that you needed to say, and think that everything is going to be okay just like that." She snapped her fingers, and if he didn't know her, he might have only heard the anger in her voice and not the hurt. "It's been years, Adam, *years*, since we did anything together. We've gone months with you barely saying anything to me. And it's been at least ten years since you included me in anything. We barely talk; you don't know me at all. You don't know anything about me anymore. And I don't know you."

There was no arguing with her. She was right. As much as he wanted to defend himself, because he'd felt like he really was doing things for her, he couldn't.

"You're right. I know. I wasn't thinking that I could waltz in here and have everything go back to normal. Whatever normal is anymore, I guess. But I was kind of hoping I could have some time to show you that I'm serious. I know almost everything that happened is my fault. And I want to make it right."

"Almost?" she asked, but she didn't sound belligerent or militant. She sounded vulnerable, like she doubted that maybe she had been making the right decision. It was the first glimmer that he had gotten that maybe she wasn't completely satisfied with what she had done.

He was taking a chance, but he was going to be honest. "I don't think there's ever just one person who's totally in the wrong. Otherwise, one of us would have been perfect. But if I had put at least as much into our marriage as you have, we wouldn't be anywhere near here."

"What could I have done?" she asked, and he heard the waver in her voice, even if he couldn't see the tears in her eyes.

He looked down, because he wasn't sure, well, he was almost sure even if she had said something, he probably wouldn't have listened. Nothing would have gotten his attention like her leaving had.

"I guess I just wish I would have had a chance to stop you before you left. To change. If somehow you could have tied me to a chair and made me listen."

"I don't think that's legal."

Was that a hint of humor in her tone? It gave him hope.

"As long as you're doing it to me, not me to you, or maybe on a consensual basis..." He didn't mean to joke about it, but it kinda came out, and she didn't glare at him. She didn't smile, but she didn't glare.

"You used to be funny," she whispered.

Man, it made him sad and made him hurt right in the middle of his chest. "I know. I lost that for a bit, being funny. I will be again. I promise. I will work on being funny."

"It wasn't something you worked on. It was just something that was natural. You smiled, and we laughed together."

As soon as she said that, she pressed her lips together, like she hadn't meant to say anything.

But that gave him an idea of one of the things she'd fallen in love with.

She was right. They hadn't had much to begin with. He had been fresh out of college, with lots of big ideas and lots of debt, since he'd bought the house and was trying to start a business.

They hadn't had to have a whole lot. They'd done a lot of holding hands and maybe sharing an ice-cream cone between them.

Back then, it was romantic to eat the same cone.

Now... Now he wanted that back. He wanted his wife back. And he wasn't afraid to work to get her. But he couldn't do it all tonight. He looked up at the sky.

"It's going to be dark soon. Is it okay if I stay? I won't come in the house, except...if I can shower?" he asked, sounding humble.

She nodded, and it wasn't exactly what he wanted in his heart, but his chest did feel a little lighter. He'd crossed the first hurdle. At least he would be able to be close to her.

He hadn't known for sure. There was always the chance that she would have said, "No, if you're staying here, I'm going to go somewhere else." Or she could have tried to keep him off their property.

He wouldn't have fought her, but just the fact that she allowed it gave him the thought that maybe it wasn't as hopeless as what he had thought it would be.

She wasn't angry. Or, if she was, it wasn't an irrational anger that had curdled into hate.

She had never been impossible to please. Never. She'd always been sweetly eager and thankful, even for something as simple as him picking up milk and bread on his way home from work.

He hadn't seen it then.

But he saw it easily now. Getting jolted the way he had hadn't been the way that he would have wanted to be yanked out of his work bubble. But in hindsight, it might have been the only way it would have worked.

"Thanks," he said and started back toward his truck.

# Chapter 10

LINDY WATCHED AS ADAM pulled some kind of big rectangular thing out of his truck and, instead of coming to the walk, started out through the yard.

When he was about fifty yards away from the house, even with the frontline of it, he set the big thing down and started unzipping it.

She'd forgotten about the teacup in her hand, and she tossed the contents out, off the side of the porch, holding the teabag back with her other hand.

She pulled out her phone and checked the time. Gage would be dropping Sierra off soon. He had offered, feeling like he owed her, since she had been stopping in Blueberry Beach on her way to the school and picking his kids up.

She wasn't keeping track, but if he felt like he owed her, she wasn't going to argue because she'd wanted to get the sign painted.

By the time she'd taken her teacup in, she'd decided that she wasn't going to take a walk. Coming back out on the porch, she watered the pansies she had sitting in planters next to the door.

She looked over, wondering what in the world Adam was doing, but it only took her a couple of seconds to realize he was setting up a tent.

Her husband was going to camp in her side yard.

It was his yard, too. He could have demanded to be in the house. But there were only two bedrooms. They had a loveseat and a recliner in the living room. Their beach house wasn't huge, just perfect for a vacation.

She supposed, if he had demanded, she could have slept on the loveseat. It wouldn't have been very comfortable.

She pulled her cheeks into her mouth and bit down.

He'd come.

She wasn't sure if she was happy about that or not.

He'd sold his business, and she couldn't believe it. She didn't want to believe it. She hadn't wanted that. It had meant so much to him, and she didn't want to ask him to give up anything. She wouldn't have. Other than a little bit of time.

It didn't seem to matter.

He was here.

He'd sold their house.

What had he done with everything inside of it?

She supposed it served her right because she'd walked away from it all, but she hadn't thought when she walked out that she'd never see any of it again. The furniture that they bought together when their business had finally been profitable. The wooden kitchen table that had been her grandparents'.

Her mother's best china.

Silverware that had been in her family for a hundred and fifty years.

She supposed it was just stuff, and that's what she'd thought when she'd left it.

Still, the idea that her house was gone had disturbed her more than she would have expected.

It was one thing to walk out of it, knowing that she could come back at any time.

It was another thing to think that someone else owned it now.

Adam hadn't even said anything to her.

She closed her eyes and took a breath. She absolutely was not going to get upset about that. She had walked away, and she had done it without saying anything to him.

It was crazy that he had sold the house that he bought, sold his business, and come after her.

She would not get upset about the house and the stuff in it.

It was just stuff.

Headlights came over the rise and up the drive. That would be Gage dropping Sierra off.

She ran inside and grabbed the small container of potato soup and a miniature loaf of bread that she'd made early that morning before the sun had dried everything up enough that she could go out and paint her sign.

The food was for Anitra, the mother whose son was ill.

She grabbed the jar of soup in one hand, the bread in the other, and pushed the door open with her hip, running down the stairs as Sierra got out of the pickup.

"Who's that, Mom?"

"Hang on a minute, honey. Let me give this to Mr. Gage." She went to the driver side as he got out.

"What's this?" he asked as he pushed the door shut.

"Soup and bread for Anitra. I thought maybe you could drop it off, if you wouldn't mind?"

"Be glad to. Where are those ladders at?"

"Hang on a second. They're in the shed, but there is no electricity. I'll have to get my phone and use it as a flashlight."

He opened his door and then took the soup and bread from her, handing it to Naomi who was sitting in the front. Lindy smiled and waved at Lexi in the back before turning and following Gage to the shed, pulling her phone out and turning the flashlight app on.

It didn't take long for them to walk to the shed and for Gage to grab one ladder while she grabbed the other.

It was a little heavy, and she had to do it in the dark because she couldn't hold the ladder and her phone at the same time, but she managed to get it out and follow Gage to the pickup.

"I could have gotten that."

"I know. But I can do it."

She didn't mind being self-sufficient. Although it was nice to be taken care of too. But Gage wasn't her husband, and it wasn't his job to take care of her.

"I'll just leave these in the back of my truck until tomorrow. What time do you think you'll be in?"

"What time suits you? Since you're helping, let's just do it on your schedule."

"I have a conference call for work right at nine o'clock, so let's make it ten thirty?" he said, taking her ladder from her and sliding it on the bed next to his.

"Sounds good." There was no way she could get her sign up without his help. "Thanks so much."

"Not a problem. See ya then."

She waved as he walked to the front of his truck, then she hurried over to the shed and closed the doors.

When she came back, Gage had backed out and started driving down the lane.

"Who was that?" Adam asked, standing by the corner of the porch, leaning against a post.

She hadn't realized he'd stopped with the tent and walked over to the house.

"A neighbor," she said, going up the steps and onto the porch.

"Is it someone I should know about?" he asked, and while his voice didn't hold anger, there might have been some jealousy there.

If he had been angry, she would have been even more so. She wasn't sure why, but she felt like after everything he'd done to her, he didn't have the right to be angry.

But he wasn't, so her tone was subdued, almost quiet. "No. That's all he is. A neighbor."

"Does the neighbor have a name?"

"Gage. His name is Gage. And he's a single dad of two girls. And he's a friend. He's given me a hand, and I've helped him, but that's it." She almost didn't say anything else, but she couldn't help it. She hadn't left Adam because she wanted anyone else. "He knows I'm married."

"Does he know you left me?"

His question was low and soft. Not mincing, just...maybe a little hurt? She wasn't sure. She was hurt herself. Hurt in a big way, because when a man loved a woman, he didn't neglect her. He didn't go for days without talking to her. He didn't put his business, his associates, his customers, and everything else he did ahead of her while he left her alone night after night.

Yeah. She was hurt.

"No. I haven't told anyone that I left you. I've just said my husband's in Pennsylvania."

He didn't say anything, then after a few moments, he pushed off the porch post. "Did you tell Sierra I'm here?"

"No. I haven't had a chance."

"I have some making up to do to her, too."

"You do."

He couldn't get back the years that he missed of his child growing up. He could only move forward and try not to make the same mistakes.

"Tomorrow. I'd like to talk to her tomorrow."

"We leave for school at seven forty-five. She'll be home by five thirty. She has practice afterwards."

"Maybe you can let her know I'd like to spend some time with her."

"I can." She didn't know whether Sierra would want to spend time with her dad or not. She didn't hate him, but she didn't really know him either.

"I guess I'm going to go to bed."

"Me too." She turned with her hand on the door.

"Are you okay?"

It was the text he sent her every night. There was concern in his voice, as there probably had been in his text.

It was a question. If she had said no, he would have come and done whatever he could to fix it.

"I'm fine," she said, the same thing she'd sent back every night.

"Good night."

"Night." She opened the screen door and walked into the house.

# Chapter 11

THE NEXT MORNING, ADAM was up before the sun. He hadn't slept very well, running over in his head the things he needed to do and trying to figure out what he *could* do.

He needed to get a job. He needed to buy some paint and some deck sealant and screws and start doing some repair work around the cottage.

That was the least of his worries. Those were things he could do, and that's what his mind wanted to fix on. The tangible. What he could put his hand to do and see get done.

But he needed to work on the more difficult and intangible problem of what to do now for his wife.

He had no idea. The more they conversed, the less stilted and awkward it felt, but she seemed suspicious. And not exceptionally happy to have him camping out in her yard.

In fact, not the slightest bit happy, even upset. Annoyed maybe.

Although, she had definitely been impressed that he'd sold his business.

He could tell that. It surprised her.

It surprised everyone who knew him. No one believed it.

But nothing was more important than his wife. If he truly believed that, he needed to live it.

Selling his business had been a big part of that.

Pastor Rendell had been right. Years of neglect weren't going to be overcome overnight with just one big gesture.

It was cold. He definitely needed more than a sleeping bag to stay warm. He'd forgotten how cold it was in Michigan. Maybe it had to do with the wind from the lake.

His tent would block some of it, but not nearly all.

Regardless, since he was awake, he might as well get up and take a walk along the beach. Maybe he could see his daughter before she left for school.

His wife was his biggest concern. But very close to that, in second place, was his daughter.

He wanted them both. He kind of thought that his daughter might be a little easier to win.

She wasn't the one who had left him.

Regardless, winning his wife would probably be the biggest step toward winning his daughter, other than time spent doing everything he needed to do. And that just took...time.

He was back by seven, and he wasn't sure whether he should hang out in his tent or sit on the porch steps until they came out for school.

He figured while they were gone, he could go in and take a shower.

Grabbing his duffel with the things he needed from his pickup, he went and sat down on the step.

He would rather face them clean, but at least he got to see them.

Although he had no idea what he was going to say.

Just sitting in the cold had been enough to cool him down from his walk, and he was close to shivering by the time the door opened.

He stood, turning.

Sierra stood on the porch, slowly moving away from the door, her eyes on him, and allowing the screen to slam behind her.

She didn't seem upset, maybe wary.

"Hey, Dad."

"Sierra. How have you been?"

She shrugged, like it didn't matter. "Fine."

He felt awkward, like he didn't even know how to talk to his own daughter. An apology wasn't going to be easy, but he might as well start there.

His stomach felt empty and hot. "I'm sorry. I...I haven't been a very good dad. I'd like a chance to do better."

She shrugged again and snapped the gum she was chewing. "Fine."

Funny how the word "fine" could mean anything but fine.

"How's the clarinet coming?"

Her eyes flew to his, and he figured she was probably surprised that he'd remembered that she played it.

He'd run into things when he had packed up the house, sheet music and such. He'd kept it. Everything was in storage in Pennsylvania.

He hadn't gotten rid of anything. He didn't know what Sierra and Lindy might want to keep and what they didn't. So he'd kept it all.

"It's fine."

"I heard they have a group for you to play in out here?"

Her gum went snap, then she blew a bubble. "They do. I'm practicing after school today."

"That sounds good."

He didn't know what else to say. He didn't know his daughter. And he didn't have anything to talk to her about.

Maybe if he'd listened to her a little bit more when she rambled on and on and on when she was younger, he might have an idea what her interests were now.

"You made some friends?"

"Yep."

The door opened again, and he looked up. Lindy, fresh cheeks and bright eyes, with her hair pulled loosely back from her face in a ponytail, wearing jacket and jeans and canvas sneakers, stepped out.

She looked beautiful, and he almost told her so.

When was the last time he'd said that to her?

It'd been a long time. He couldn't even remember.

He didn't say it now. It would sound like he was trying to score points. Even though his eyes ran all over her, knowing that the chasm between him and the lady standing in front of him was almost entirely his fault.

Maybe Lindy could have tried harder to talk to him. But she was so laid-back and easygoing she always would let him get away with more than he should have.

He could hardly fault her for not being more assertive.

"I assumed you were going to take a shower while we are gone?" she said as she stepped out behind her daughter. Sierra moved, going down the stairs past him and walking to the car.

"If that's okay."

"It is," she said with no expression on her face. He couldn't tell if she cared or not. "I don't have your soap or shampoo or anything."

"It's fine." He almost said he'd use hers, although he had brought his own.

He just wanted to smell the smell that was hers. He'd missed it.

He loved taking a shower after she did. She made the bathroom smell heavenly. Wherever she walked, she left a trail of good scents. Funny the things he missed, but that was most definitely one of them.

He could tell she'd been there, just by smelling her.

She moved by him, and he caught her scent, breathing deep, closing his eyes, thinking about the things he didn't appreciate when he had them.

"I'll be in town for a bit," she threw over her shoulder as she walked down the stairs.

He clenched his jaw. He had no right to be upset. The way he was when he'd seen the other man pulling in last night and Lindy hurrying out to greet him, like she might have done with him a time long ago. Smiling and laughing and chatting. It had torn him up inside.

He'd wondered if he'd come too late.

The idea that she might have left him for someone else hadn't occurred to him. She'd said in her letter that she hadn't, and he believed her.

Of course, he'd not thought that she might have found someone else. Not until last evening when that pickup had pulled in and she'd gone running to it.

It scared him. Deeply. His own faults, he might be able to overcome those, but if she'd fallen in love with someone else... He didn't think he stood a chance. She already knew what he did—married her, took advantage of her, and then neglected her.

How could he convince her that he could be anything better than anyone else who came along? As long as the guy didn't beat her and didn't yell at her, he pretty much had Adam beat from the start.

He'd been such a fool.

Last night, for the first time, he'd altered the prayer that he'd been praying every night and most of the day since Lindy had walked out—asking the Lord to give him the wisdom he needed to win his wife back.

Last night for the first time, he thought to ask the Lord to turn her heart toward his and keep her from looking at anyone else.

He hadn't thought Lindy was that kind of woman. She might have left him, but he'd thought she would never break the vows she'd made.

But he had to admit he didn't really know her. And she'd almost assuredly been lonely. And hungry for not just attention but affection. He hadn't been affectionate, hadn't given her the attention she deserved and almost certainly needed.

He stood on the porch watching until they left, pulling out the lane and disappearing over the rise.

He had been at the beach house plenty of times on vacation, at least once a year. Although two years ago, Lindy had come out by herself, because he just couldn't pull himself away from the business. One of his best employees had quit, and he had jobs lined up for months out, and he couldn't afford to go down two people. So he told her to go ahead and go by herself.

She had.

It hadn't occurred to him until recently that maybe she hadn't wanted to go on vacation without her husband. And maybe he shouldn't have kept encouraging her to do things by herself, because it made it that much easier for her to leave him. By herself.

He turned, opening the door and stepping in. Her familiar scent hit him when he walked in. He'd missed it. Missed the little touches she had everywhere. Some lace at the windows, a couple of throw pillows that were pretty against the beige loveseat. A butterfly magnet on the refrigerator. The bed neatly made in the bedroom, even down to the little pillow shaped like a starfish that decorated the top of it.

The bathroom smelled familiar and beloved. The scent of his wife.

He hadn't cried when she left. Hadn't even thought about it. And he'd been busy ever since, working hard to get where he was right now.

And now, he had nothing to do.

Nothing but to try to figure out what in the world he could do that would convince her that he would never do what he'd been doing for the last fifteen years again.

Maybe it was her scent, maybe it was the memories of them being happy at the beach house, maybe it was the idea that there was another man and everything he'd been working for was for naught—a thought that scared him to the very marrow of his bones—maybe it was just the fact that everything on his agenda had been taken care of, and that left only one thing. The hardest thing. Winning his wife.

Whatever it was, he didn't even realize he was crying until he dropped his duffel and knelt beside the edge of the tub, his forehead on the rim, breathing in her scent, as the tears streamed down his cheeks.

# Chapter 12

AFTER LINDY DROPPED Sierra off at school, she drove back to Blueberry Beach and parked her car, walking to the diner.

She didn't know what to do. She had left Adam, thinking that was the end of it. Thinking he would go on with his business, and she would leave, and eventually, he would find someone to replace her and ask for a divorce.

Not that that's what she wanted, but she just assumed it was the way it would go. Maybe he'd never find anyone. After all, he hadn't had time for her; he shouldn't have time for anyone else. She supposed she hadn't really thought about it.

He wasn't supposed to show up here. He wasn't supposed to sell his business. He wasn't supposed to sell their house, for goodness' sake.

She smiled at Iva May as she gave her order for coffee.

"No turkey sandwich?" Iva May asked with a smile.

"No. Thank you."

Normally, she was a little friendlier, but she was having a hard time faking it.

Iva May took her money and gave her change.

She took her coffee from Iva May, went to the table in the far back, and sat down. She didn't have a particular table she sat at, because sometimes the diner was busy. But she preferred to sit by the window if she could.

It wasn't full today, but she'd chosen the table she was least likely to be seen at. Not that there was much room to hide.

She sat with her back to the diner, facing the wall.

That was why she was surprised when Iva May walked over and said, "May I sit down?"

Lindy tried to smile, and she nodded. "Sure."

She and Iva May had talked a good bit over the last six weeks. Bill, the man who owned the surf shop, along with Dr. Chambers, who manned the griddle in the mornings when the diner opened from five until seven, had also become people she considered her friends.

As had Beverly, who wasn't a business owner in Blueberry Beach but, from what Lindy understood from the others, was significantly wealthy and had contributed money not only to start the hospital in Blueberry Beach but to keep it running and also to open the new oncology wing.

Dr. Chambers was in charge of setting up the protocols and training the new doctors for the new wing.

Lindy hadn't quite figured out why Dr. Chambers was in the diner in the morning other than the slight connection of Anitra having a child with cancer. He hadn't grown up in the town. She did know that much.

Several other business owners up and down the street often sat together in the diner chatting, on Saturdays especially.

She'd gotten to know them quite well, especially Iva May. She almost felt like a mother to her.

Iva May sat down across from her. Her old wrinkled hand patted Lindy's. "I know there's something bothering you. You don't have to tell me if you don't want to. But I thought I'd just come over and be a silent support, if you don't want to share."

"Thanks," Lindy said a little dejectedly.

"There must be something on your mind, honey."

She hadn't told anyone what had been going on between Adam and her. She just said her husband was in Pennsylvania. Of course, that raised some eyebrows, since she was leasing a spot along Main Street and putting a business in.

She should be working on that. Not that there was much to do. The ice cream was in the cooler, and the coolers were on. The candy was stocked on the shelves, and everything was ready for opening day. All she needed to do was put the sign up when Gage got there at 10:30.

It wouldn't hurt to run over the books again or to get used to the software that the previous owner had been using.

She'd been very blessed to have that phone number and to get those contacts with the vendors. It would have been a lot harder without them. But everything seemed to fall in place.

It felt like the hand of the Lord, but it couldn't be, because she knew He wouldn't bless what she'd done.

Leaving her husband was never right.

She sighed and looked at Iva May. "I left my husband. I guess you probably figured that out."

Iva May did not look surprised, but compassion seemed to ooze from her, warm and soft. "I suspected."

"He didn't cheat. Neither did I. It was just...he never paid attention to me. I know that sounds childish. But I'm serious. We didn't talk. He didn't even know I was home. He never talked to our daughter. He had no time for us."

"Is he an alcoholic?"

"No. A workaholic. Which is probably maybe not as heartbreaking, but just as bad."

"I see."

Iva May seemed so kind and caring. The words just started falling from Lindy's lips.

"He lived for his job. And it used to be, when we were first married, that I helped him. But when he moved his office out of the house and I couldn't go with him because of our daughter, I kind of got left behind. And maybe it was partly my fault because I only tried to say something once in a while..."

"It's hard."

"That's right. I didn't want to start a fight. I didn't want to confront him. So I kind of tried to hint about it. But he didn't get my hints."

"You tried to tell him you were lonely?"

"No. I couldn't tell him that."

"Why not?"

"Because he would say 'why don't you go and do something?'"

"Why didn't you?"

"I did! I went out. I got a job. I did things. Every time I asked him to do something with me, he would say 'you go ahead and do it, I'm busy.'"

"Oh. I see."

"Yeah. I mean just something simple, like 'let's go for ice cream.' And he would say 'you go ahead. I'm busy.' I would sit out on the porch on summer evenings, and he would sit inside and work." Lindy bit the insides of her cheeks. "I guess I could have gone in and sat down at the table beside him."

"I suppose you could have."

"But he probably wouldn't have known I was there. The very few times that he would talk to me, he would interrupt our conversation if his phone rang. He would answer it. Like we were in the middle of a conversation—I might be telling him about our daughter—and he would just answer his phone."

"Well, he did have to keep his business going."

"I know. I know. But Saturday, Sunday, evenings, mornings, didn't matter. There was no time that I could talk to him that his phone wouldn't interrupt us."

"I see."

"He didn't care to go anywhere with me. It was like he didn't like me." Her voice cracked, and she hated that. She had sworn to herself that she wasn't going to cry anymore. She was done. He wasn't going to have the power to hurt her with his neglect.

"Oh. You felt like he didn't love you because..."

"Yes. Because we didn't have a relationship. I mean, what was the point in being married?"

"I see. There was no point. And you felt neglected and unloved because even though he probably felt like he was providing for you and taking good care of you, it wasn't how you felt?"

"Yeah. I guess. Something like that."

"And you didn't tell him."

"No. Should I have?"

Iva May moved the silverware around that was sitting in front of her. "You mean you left without saying anything?"

"I felt like he had a choice about what he could do. He could choose to work, or he could choose to spend time with me. And he always chose work. I tried to hint. Sometimes, I would text and say 'hey, there's a new restaurant opening,' or 'would you like to meet somewhere for lunch,' or sometimes, I asked him straight out to do something with me. But I quit. Because his answer was always no."

"So you left."

"Yeah. I got laid off my job—I was a store supervisor of a candy store in town, and it closed. He didn't even know. I was laid off for six weeks, and he didn't even know that I didn't go to work."

"I see."

"Yeah." Lindy pressed her lips together and fiddled with the coffee she hadn't drunk. She hadn't even taken a sip. She didn't feel like eating or drinking anything. "And now he's here in Blueberry Beach."

Iva May was quiet for a moment, digesting that information. "I've noticed that you've lost weight since you came here."

"Yeah."

"Your hair has gotten lighter, and you've got a tan."

"I suppose I do look a little different. Not that he's said anything or noticed. He never looked at me before. He wouldn't notice if I changed now."

"If he's here, that should mean something? How long is he here for?"

"That's just it. He sold the business. He sold it." She spread her hands out on the table, trying to convey what a big deal that was. "The thing that meant more to him than anything in the world—he sold it and our house. Yesterday, he drove in and set up a tent in our yard. He's here to stay."

"You don't sound happy about that."

"I'm not. Not really. Maybe ten years ago, that would have thrilled my soul that he wanted me, but I spent the last ten years convincing myself that it didn't matter until I really feel like it doesn't. I was happy by myself. Not that I want anyone else, although I am lonely..."

"He's the only one that you can go to."

"I know. I don't want anyone else. Why would I? Marriage is terrible."

"Maybe it's your attitude."

"My fault? Is it my fault, really?"

"No. It's not your fault that he neglected you and ignored you, although you could have been more assertive, and I think you know that."

"Yeah. I guess I could have had fights about it."

"It might have worked."

"Maybe."

"At least he would have known where you stood and what you wanted."

"I don't think it's rocket science to figure out that your wife wants to spend time with you. That she doesn't want to be relegated to the very bottom of your list. Something that you never get to."

"You're right. But if he sold his business? And your house? And he's moved out? Maybe he wants another chance," Iva May suggested slowly.

That was exactly what she'd thought. It seemed obvious. "Maybe I don't want to give him another chance. Maybe I don't want to go through that again. Maybe that hurts." Even just saying it made her chest pinch and burn and her nose tingle. She wasn't going to cry. She wasn't.

"Yeah. We're all afraid of pain."

Lindy hadn't really thought about being afraid. But it was probably true. She was afraid of being hurt again. That was why she wasn't happy to see her husband pull up. Why she wasn't happy to see him in their yard. Why she didn't want to take the olive branch that he had extended and see if they could work something out.

She was happy to just be apart from him so she wasn't hurting anymore.

She sighed. "Fear. I guess, I guess if I don't try to work it out or at least meet my husband halfway, I'm letting fear control me?"

"You were hurt; he wasn't. There's a difference," Iva May pointed out.

She supposed that was right. Of course, her husband hadn't been hurt. Not all those years that she'd been alone and hurting.

Of course, he wanted another chance. He wasn't afraid of getting hurt again.

"He's made himself vulnerable to you. Hasn't he? He sold what was keeping him and came out and, I assume, asked permission to set up a tent?"

Lindy nodded. "Yeah. He asked."

"Do you think, if you had said no, that he would have not set it up? Would he have left?"

Lindy thought about that; she didn't really know. But maybe she did. This new Adam was different in a lot of ways, but he was still the same man of character.

"I think so. I think he would have left. I mean, I never thought of saying no. It's his ground too. But I think if I had told him he couldn't stay..." She shrugged.

"He made himself vulnerable to you. You could have said no, and that would have been a rejection he deserved."

That was all well and good, and probably true, but it didn't solve the actual problem.

She threw her hands up. "What do I do? I don't want this in my life. I was happy. I was getting started running a business, happy on the beach, just no more stress and worry, wondering whether he was finally going to notice me tonight, or going to bed and crying myself to sleep because he didn't. I'm just over it. I'm so over it." She dropped her hands and wanted to drop her head along with them. It made her tired and sad just thinking about it.

"Only you know whether you value your marriage and the vows you made enough to let yourself be vulnerable to getting hurt again. Because it's a possibility. Does he normally not keep his word?"

That was an easy question. "No, he's honest. I would trust him with anything."

"Then ask him what his intentions are. And then ask him to make a promise. Whatever you can live with to make you willing to try again."

Lindy bit her lip, nodding slowly. Adam wouldn't make a promise that he wasn't sure he could keep. Or, if he made a promise, he would die trying to keep it.

That's what he was actually doing. He'd made vows and apparently realized that he wasn't keeping them, and now he was trying.

"I think I can trust him."

"It's hard to hand your heart back over to someone once it's been hurt." Iva May's wise voice was filled with compassion and no judgment.

"Yeah. It is."

The bell jingled, and Iva May looked up. "I've got a customer. Are you going to be okay?"

Lindy nodded. "I'm meeting Gage in a few minutes, and we're going to put my sign up. Opening is on Saturday." She smiled, deliberately trying to shove all those other things aside and look happy. She really *was* happy about Blueberry Candy Cream. Her own shop. She loved the sound of it.

"I can't wait to see it hanging on the street. If I can break away from here for a few minutes, I'd like to take a picture of you underneath it."

"I'd love that."

Iva May stood up, but before she walked away, she leaned over, slipping her arm around Lindy's shoulders and giving her a warm coffee-scented hug. "It is a blessing to have you in the store every day. I'll pray that everything works out for you. And you make wise decisions."

"Thank you. That makes me feel better. Honestly. I know I should love my husband. And I've been afraid to pray about it."

"Don't be afraid. God loves you. And He doesn't want to see you hurt any more than you want to be hurt. Of course, He does want you to do right."

"I know." She grinned a little, squeezing and returning Iva May's hug. "Thanks for listening to me. And for giving me good advice. I know you're right."

"Even with the risk of hurting in the long run, you'll never regret doing the right thing."

"True. Thanks."

She waited until Iva May left before she picked up her undrunk coffee and threw it in the garbage can. With renewed determination, she gave Iva May a little wave as she walked out the door and across the street in order to meet Gage.

# Chapter 13

IT COULD ONLY BE THE Lord, since Adam had gotten into town just as the owner of the surf shop was putting a "help wanted" sign in his window.

He'd walked in and asked about it. The surf shop owner, Bill, had said that the job might not be full-time hours, and he couldn't offer benefits at first, but he'd hire Adam anyway even though he had no experience and didn't know a thing about surfing.

Adam figured it was probably a fair trade. Bill explained that they didn't really surf on Lake Michigan, but he did sell wet suits and surfboards. Boogie boards were his biggest seller, along with other water and sports equipment—volleyball nets, badminton, even cricket.

The store wasn't busy, and after Adam filled out some paperwork, Bill showed him the ropes.

Adam had been upfront with Bill and let him know that this wasn't something he intended to do for the rest of his life, but he wouldn't leave him in the lurch.

"That's fine," Bill said. "I really only need someone because I've been helping my neighbor across the street. Anitra, who owns the diner, is having a hard time of it right now, her son has cancer." Bill wasn't too much older than Adam—maybe a decade—his hair was thinning, just like Adam's, and his waist thickening, too. Adam felt an immediate kinship with him. He assumed it must be a little mutual since Bill had hired him on the spot. "All the shop owners on the street have gotten together along with a few other people and are making sure she stays open for business during the busy season."

"Wow. That's nice. You're actually hiring someone for your shop so you can go help her?"

"Yeah. It's a little easier to stand behind the cash register and sell boogie boards than it is to figure out how to cook an egg-white omelet with spinach and feta cheese."

"Sounds fancy. I didn't realize the diner served stuff like that." They'd been in a few times over the years when they'd vacationed, but he didn't remember much about it. He'd probably been too busy working to pay attention.

"She serves regular stuff too. But she gets a lot of folks in, more than we used to, I suppose, that want stuff like that. Maybe because of the hospital. They want their eggs to be organic, their meat organic and grass fed, and they're a little pickier."

"Guess that's the way things are going." Adam hadn't really thought about it. He wasn't in the food industry, and as long as it didn't eat him, he was pretty happy to eat it. Vegetable or meat.

He thought he'd been doing a good job of being casual, although he had seen Lindy's car in the parking lot at the end of the street, and he figured she was around somewhere.

Maybe she was meeting that man again.

He had to shut that voice down before it caused problems.

Several people walked into the shop. Bill greeted them by name, chatting and selling them a couple of beach towels, although he warned them that the water would be freezing this time of year. They assured him that they were just using them to lie on the beach.

It sounded like Bill knew a good many people. Adam figured he might know Lindy. It wouldn't hurt to ask.

"See?" Bill said as the door closed behind them. "Pretty simple. Every once in a while, the cash register throws a code, and sometimes, people's cards are declined. I can tell you what will happen and what you need to do, but it will help for you to experience it."

Adam nodded. He'd worked all his life but never behind a cash register, and he watched and listened while Bill showed him the various buttons and explained some issues he might run into.

Fifteen minutes later, no one else had come in. Bill suggested he come around so he could show him the stuff in the back that would need to be shelved.

While they were walking back, Adam said, "Do you know Lindy?"

"A woman?" Bill raised a brow, and his expression wasn't exactly suspicious, but it wasn't as open as before.

"Yeah." Adam resisted the urge to fidget. "Her name is Lindy."

"Is she tall, blondish hair, nice lady about your age?"

"Yeah." He described Lindy perfectly, and Adam felt his hopes lift.

"What is she to you?" Bill's eyes narrowed, and his stance became less open and more suspicious.

Adam figured his question probably seemed out of bounds, and maybe Bill would think he was a stalker.

He held both hands up. "I'm her husband."

Bill, who was slightly taller than him, seemed to look way, way down at him. "That's funny. She never mentioned a husband."

"She left me."

"You beat her?"

"No!"

Adam really didn't want to talk about it, but he also knew that Bill was protecting Lindy, which he actually did appreciate. He should thank the man, although Bill was probably only ten or fifteen years older than he was.

He supposed... He narrowed his eyes at Bill, trying to size him up. He had no idea how to look at him through a woman's eyes. Was the guy handsome?

Adam didn't know. He didn't figure Lindy probably cared about that anyway. She just wanted someone who was nice and would treat her well.

Adam hadn't even been able to live up to that low standard.

"I didn't beat her, I'm not an alcoholic. I wasn't abusive in any way." He looked down, his hand going into his pocket. "Except I neglected her. I got involved in building my business and got consumed by that, and she got left by the wayside."

Man, he hated admitting it. Was ashamed.

He lifted his shoulder. "My daughter Sierra...same thing."

"That's an interesting story," Bill said, looking more suspicious than he had before Adam had said anything. He should have kept his mouth shut.

"So I sold my business, sold our house in Pennsylvania, and last night, she let me set up a tent in the side yard of our beach cottage."

Bill's lips twitched. "Dude? You set up a tent in the yard of your own beach cottage?"

Adam pressed his lips together, not wanting to be the laughing-stock of Blueberry Beach but knowing he deserved it. He nodded. "Yeah." In case Bill missed it, he said, "That's how bad I want her back."

The suspicion on Bill's face was completely gone. "Gotta say, that's a pretty big gesture, but I'm on the lady's side. If she doesn't want you, you need to accept that."

"I know."

The idea was inconceivable. He'd have to accept it, he knew. He would have no choice. He couldn't make her do anything. Like Pastor Rendell had said, he could only change himself. Then he could hope and pray that Lindy would see that he was sincere and accept him.

"She'll either make her decision for me or against me." He hesi-tated, then figured he had nothing to lose. "Maybe you could answer one question for me?" Bill lifted a brow but didn't make any promises. "There was some guy at our beach house last night. He left with ladders, but she ran out to him looking pretty happy to see him...do I have com-petition?" he asked, forcing himself to meet Bill's eyes, because the eas-ier thing to do would be to stare at the floor.

It was humbling to ask a complete stranger that he'd only just met that day whether or not his wife was seeing another man.

"That was probably Gage. I heard him saying yesterday in the diner that he was going to help her put her sign up. I would assume that would take ladders."

"Sign?"

"You really don't know your wife, do you?"

"I told you. She left me."

"Don't you have her number? Did you think about, you know, giving her a call? Shoot the breeze or something?"

"I texted her every night, but I figured she probably didn't want to talk to me. I hadn't made time for her for a long time. She probably didn't want to walk out the door and all of a sudden have me call her every day."

"Then I don't know how in the Sam Hill you think you're going to win her back without talking to her?"

"I had to take care of my business first, had to take care of the house, had to get rid of all of that stuff, so all I had to focus on was her. I don't want to have to put her aside again."

"Yeah. Good luck with that." Bill kinda smirked, but Adam thought maybe he was a little more sympathetic to his plight, since he'd been as open as he could be and had totally humbled himself.

A man couldn't get much lower than admitting that his wife had left him, and it was all his fault, just because he was stupid.

Bill turned back toward the shelf, like he didn't really want to talk about Lindy anymore, although he had seemed to know something about a sign, and it must be in town, since her car was there.

But Bill didn't seem to indicate that she was having any kind of fling with that Gage person, which was a relief.

They worked for another hour, with Bill showing him everything he needed to do to get started. When they were done, Bill told him his hours would be from eight to two to start. Bill would come in after helping serve breakfast and lunch at the diner.

Adam thanked him, went to his pickup, and drove home, eager to get there since Lindy's car wasn't parked where it had been earlier that day.

Maybe she would be home. Although, he didn't know what he would say to her. And didn't know what to do to win her back. He'd already given up everything—not that he needed special accolades for that, he just wasn't sure what else he could do.

He fingered the booklet in his pocket that he hadn't gone anywhere without since the pastor had given it to him. Maybe it was time for him to give Pastor Rendell another call. After all, he supposed a man probably needed help when he couldn't figure out what in the world he could say to his wife.

# Chapter 14

LINDY TRIED TO FIX the broken shutter, holding it up with her knee while she put the screw in and tried to line it up with one hand while moving the shutter up and down with her other.

It was just tall enough that her arms got tired reaching up, and she kept having to take a break and hadn't been able to get the screw lined up with the hole already there.

She probably should get a stool. But she had thought it would just be a couple-minute task, and she didn't want to take the time to find something to stand on, since Gage still had the ladders on the back of his truck. He had said he would bring them out when the girls got done at practice this evening.

She didn't want to wait and had thought this would be a quick fix.

She should have known better.

She was still unsuccessfully trying to move it up and down when the sound of a car motor made her turn her head and her husband's truck came over the rise. She'd seen it sitting in town when she got in her car to leave after Gage had helped her put her sign up. She had thanked him and walked around her store, checking for the millionth time that everything was ready.

She was excited but also apprehensive.

She hadn't sunk her entire savings into it, but she spent more than she felt comfortable with.

She didn't have the buffer she should have started out with. But she was taking a risk. And she supposed that in order to get anywhere in life, that's what one had to do.

That's what happened when one stood in front of a preacher and looked into the eyes of the person they claimed to love and pledged their life to them.

It was a risk.

She'd taken a risk and lost on Adam.

Except...he seemed to want to reconcile. Although he hadn't said it in so many words.

Iva May seemed to indicate that even though she knew she could get hurt again, it was probably best to try.

She wanted to. Deep down, she knew she wanted to. That Iva May was right. The thing that was holding her back was fear. Fear of the pain. She'd been through it once.

From the sound of his motor, Adam parked beside her car where he'd been last night. He got out of his pickup immediately, slamming the door shut. It sounded like he took the steps onto the porch two at a time.

Without greeting her, he grabbed a hold of the bottom of the shutter, brushing her fingers with his, and she pulled her hand away quickly.

He took the top, not commenting on touching her nor her reaction, and guided it up and down as she held the screw in the hole, trying to line them up.

"There's a hole in the wood underneath?" he asked, his voice mellow.

"Yes. I checked it before I started lining them up. And the screw fits."

The shutters were just for show. Maybe at one time, they had been working shutters, but when they had bought the house, the shutters were screwed onto the wood siding.

"A little farther up, I think," she said.

He complied without saying anything.

He smelled familiar and safe, and it stirred feelings she preferred not to have to deal with as the screw finally found its hole.

She said, "Hold it," and screwed it in, lifting the screwdriver to finish the job.

"This was one of the things I was going to get to this afternoon."

"Well, I beat ya," she said, hearing that there wasn't much friendliness in her voice, but it wasn't cold either.

She finished tightening the screw, and they both stepped back, her holding the screwdriver and him looking at her with an expression she couldn't read.

Regret? Longing? She didn't think so. It almost seemed like there was desire in his gaze, but she hardly thought that could be true.

The idea was almost laughable.

"Well, thanks. I appreciate your help." She shoved the screwdriver in her pocket and slapped her hands together, getting ready to turn away.

She froze when he spoke. "Lindy... I..."

She faced the lake, looking out on its broad blue expanse, glistening in the sunlight. Warming under the heat. Beautiful, ever changing, and comforting.

She didn't say anything. She wasn't sure she wanted to listen to him.

He cleared his throat. "I... Sierra told me she had practice after school today. I thought maybe I could pick her up, take her out to eat. Maybe to the diner in town."

"It closes at three," she said. Not meaning to be short, but she was.

She wasn't sure whether Sierra would be happy or not to go with her dad. But she could hardly tell Adam he couldn't see his daughter. That wasn't her intention at all.

"Well then, where do you suggest we go?"

She lifted her shoulder. "I don't know. I think there's a couple of fast-food restaurants over toward the hospital. I haven't been over that way much. But as I recall, they were building them last summer when I was here." Maybe she did mean to emphasize that he hadn't been around even if he had gone on vacation with them.

"Yes. I remember. It looked like they were putting more than a few things in there on that road beside the hospital."

"Yeah. You could try there."

"I guess I will then, if that's okay."

"Gage was actually going to pick them up. He has my ladders, and he was bringing them back tonight."

"Gage is the man who was here before?"

"Yep." She crossed her arms over her chest. She had nothing to hide. Had done nothing wrong. Maybe she should be more sympathetic to him, but it was hard. She didn't want to be hurt again.

"So are you telling me that you don't want me to pick Sierra up?" His voice still held no irritation, but it was maybe a little more insecure.

"No. I'll have to call Gage and let him know you'll be doing it."

"Do you want me to get the ladders from him? I can bring them home."

She wasn't sure she liked this Adam. This person who was asking her permission for everything. Who seemed to expect her to be in charge.

She didn't want to be in charge.

She just didn't want to be marginalized either.

"I guess you can if you want." She turned to look at him, although she could hardly stand to. He looked miserable.

If she didn't know better, she'd almost say he'd been crying. His eyes were bloodshot, anyway. Probably he wasn't sleeping very well in the tent.

It had been cold at night, and she thought of him more than once. But what could she do? Short of inviting him in. And then she'd have to sleep on the loveseat, which would mean she would be the one not getting any sleep.

"I want."

"Okay then. I'll text him and let him know."

"Thanks. Can I do anything else for you?"

"No thank you. I'm fine." She turned, putting her hand on the screen door's knob and opening it. "I've got some things to do inside."

"Okay. See you."

"Yeah." She opened the door and walked in.

# Chapter 15

ADAM MADE IT TO SIERRA'S practice early.

He figured it couldn't hurt and hoped to get a chance to maybe listen a little.

Lindy hadn't said a word, but along with neglecting her, he'd done the same to his daughter and had missed a lot.

He figured he couldn't make it up to anyone, but maybe he could start today to be better.

He stopped at Bill's store for a couple of minutes on his way through, and then he grabbed a few sandwiches from the fast-food joint, hoping he wasn't taking too much for granted.

Sierra might not want to have anything to do with him.

The kids were practicing outside, and he parked far enough away that he wasn't a distraction.

He got out of his truck and walked over to where the kids were practicing, staying to the side so they didn't see him.

He didn't recognize any of the songs, but it looked like the kids were having fun, and between numbers, there was a lot of laughing.

There were about ten kids in the group, and only two were boys.

Sierra wasn't hanging out with any of the boys, but she talked a good bit to two girls, who, unless Adam missed his guess, were probably sisters. They looked almost exactly alike.

One was slightly shorter than the other one.

When the leader said they could put their instruments away, the kids moseyed over to the nearby benches where the cases were. Adam strolled over, walking up to the director and holding out his hand.

"I'm Adam Coates, Sierra's father."

She was an older woman with kindly eyes that were lively and a quick smile that made her face wrinkle, and he liked that, because he figured it meant she used her smile a lot. "I'm Mrs. Hershey. Rebecca Hershey. And I'm pleased to meet you. Sierra is a lot of fun, and she's really enjoying this. She has a lot of talent on the clarinet."

"Thanks. She must get it from her mom. Sometimes, I can't even play the radio in tune."

Mrs. Hershey laughed, a sound that was at once joyful and carefree, and he liked her immediately. "Well, your daughter definitely has a good bit of musical ability. Of course, a lot of whether or not someone learns to play an instrument, and how well, really depends on how much work and time they're willing to put into it. She must practice a lot. Sometimes, it can be hard to be consistent." Mrs. Hershey said it as a statement, but her brows kinda lifted like she was waiting for him to agree.

He almost did. But that wouldn't have been right. He had no idea whether she practiced or not. "I haven't been home much lately, and, I'll just have to be honest, I don't know whether she practices or not."

The smile faded from her face, and her brows drew down. He'd known she would think less of him, if he said the honest thing, but he didn't see any point in lying.

Lying never got anyone anywhere, and it wasn't right.

"I see." Mrs. Hershey seemed to recover her smile. "Well, you're here today. So I think that's a good thing."

"I hope so. I hope she's happy to see me."

That made her brows shoot skyward, but another parent was walking over, and he nodded at Mrs. Hershey before he walked to his daughter.

"Hi, Sierra," he said, hating that he sounded a little insecure. He wanted to be confident, but he honestly wasn't sure whether she would even acknowledge him, let alone talk to him.

"Hey, Dad," she said, not sounding super thrilled to see him, but at least she didn't snub him.

"Are these the friends you were talking about?"

"Yep. That's Lexi, and that's Naomi." He couldn't really tell which one was which, since Sierra kind of tilted her head and didn't really look at him as she snapped her clarinet case closed and grabbed the handle.

"Hi, Naomi. Hi, Lexi, whichever one is which," he said.

They giggled, and the taller one held out her hand. "I'm Naomi. It's good to meet you, Mr. Coates."

"It's nice to meet you, too, Naomi. High school was a long time ago for me, but I think I have enough brainpower to figure out that if you're Naomi, you must be Lexi."

Lexi smiled, seeming to be a little bit more shy than her sister. Maybe a little younger. "Hey, Mr. Coates."

"I'm picking Sierra up, but I wanted to talk to your dad, girls. Apparently, he has some ladders for us?"

"Yeah. I guess that he has them in the back of his pickup. That's where they were this morning when he dropped us off at school," Naomi said, snapping her instrument case closed, which was bigger than Sierra's, but he hadn't really paid attention to what she was playing. Maybe a trumpet.

"He's just pulling in," Lexi said, snapping her case shut, too. It was smaller than Sierra's. He was pretty sure it was a flute.

"That's great." He turned to Sierra, who was looking like she wanted to talk to her friends but closed her mouth when he spoke. "If it's okay with you, I picked up a couple of sandwiches for us at the drive-through, and I'd like to have a picnic with you on the beach. Maybe ride bikes some if you want."

Well, she didn't start smiling and jumping up and down and screaming "yeah, hey, that's exactly what I've always wanted to do," but at least she didn't scrunch up her eyes and say "no, I don't ride bikes."

Instead, she said, "Sandwiches? And bikes and a picnic?"

His stomach clenched. "That's kind of what I was thinking. Yeah."

"That's weird."

He deserved that, he supposed.

"We don't have to if you don't want to. But I just missed you and wanted to spend some time together."

Her lowered brow and unhappy face didn't get any better at that admission, and she didn't return the sentiment, but she didn't refuse him either.

"If you don't mind waiting while I talk to Lexi and Naomi's father?"

"Sure. I'll just hang out with them until you're done."

"Thanks."

Gage brought his pickup to a stop, and Adam walked over.

"Hey, Gage, I'm Adam, Lindy's husband."

Gage's eyes, which were crinkled in a friendly smile, clouded over as he realized who Adam was. Adam didn't really think it was a jealous clouding over; it was more of a "you haven't been in the picture much, and I'm not sure what you're doing here, but I'm on your wife's side" clouding over. Very similar to the emotion Bill had expressed.

Of course, Lindy had only been in Blueberry Beach six weeks, and everybody was already on her side.

Maybe that should have made him angry or frustrated, but it kinda felt like that was just the way Lindy was. Sweet and friendly and totally authentic, and people responded to that and loved her for it.

"I'm Gage." Gage held out his hand, and Adam shook it.

"If you don't mind, I can take the ladders that you have. I was picking up Sierra, and I'll just take them home with me." He kinda smirked in his head at the word "home."

After all, he was living in a tent in the yard. But Gage didn't need to know that. He'd seen the tent, but he didn't know that's where Adam was sleeping.

Unless Lindy had told him.

"Sure. I'll just pull over to your truck." He lifted his brows as though asking where that was.

Adam jerked his head at where he'd parked—a good hundred yards away, at the other end of the school.

Gage said, "I'll have to make a loop around, because it's one way through here."

"That's fine. I'll start walking up."

Gage jerked his head, called out to his girls that he'd be going around and he'd meet them up there, and pulled away.

Adam started walking, and for the first time, it occurred to him to wonder where Gage's wife was.

He had the two girls, and he'd been at Lindy's house and helped Lindy with her sign. There hadn't been any sign of a wife. Had Lindy said something about him being a single dad? Adam almost thought she might have, but he'd been more focused on an unknown man coming to his house than on the fine details. Perhaps he should have paid more attention. Though he wasn't overly curious. Whatever Gage did was his business. And Adam didn't really care as long as he left Adam's wife alone.

They didn't talk much as Gage pulled alongside Adam's pickup. Adam had the first ladder moved before Gage got out of his truck and had started on the second. Gage gave him a hand with that, and they set it in the back of Adam's pickup together.

"Those look like two of the bikes that were in the back of Bill's store, that he used to rent along the boardwalk."

"They are. I bought them from Bill yesterday."

"Really?" Gage asked with genuine interest. "You thinking about setting up a rental? You could probably do it from Lindy's store."

Adam had been doing a pretty good job of being unemotional and friendly but not too friendly. At that comment, though, his mouth hung open, and his eyes bugged out.

Lindy had a store?

Of course, he didn't know. He hadn't been talking to his wife.

"I take it from that expression that I've either surprised you with the idea of a bike rental or you didn't know your wife had a store."

"Yeah." Adam said, not really interested in talking about his personal life with a complete stranger. He'd already done it once with Bill. He didn't need to go baring his heart to every man he met. That would just be weird.

Gage waited maybe a beat or two, but then he said, "I guess I'll be seeing you around."

"I guess."

Adam didn't know why he would unless he ended up picking Sierra up from the school.

Although he supposed the girls were friends, and he might see Gage that way.

Gage almost looked like he was going to ask another question, but then he closed his mouth, called out to his girls, and walked to his pickup, getting in with a friendly wave goodbye.

Sierra had come over when Gage called his girls, and she threw her book bag in the back before she got in the front of his pickup. "Where'd you get the bikes from?"

"Mr. Bill had them in the back of his store. I bought them."

"Really? I didn't know Mr. Bill had bikes."

"Actually, he had a bunch of them. Twelve that are able to be used, a couple more that have broken pedals, and one that has a broken chain. A lot of them need air in the tires."

"What are you going to do with twelve bikes?" She eyed him across the seat. "Do you have kids I don't know about?"

At least she was talking to him.

"I was thinking about a bike rental. Apparently, your mom has a store."

Sierra looked at him like that was common knowledge and something that a husband should most definitely know about his wife. He couldn't say he disagreed with her, but he couldn't help it. He was doing the best he could, but he was playing catch-up right now.

"She does. It's going to be a candy store, and I got to name it."

She'd managed a candy store in Pennsylvania. It made sense that she would open one here. With her experience, she'd probably do really well. "What's the name you chose?"

"Blueberry Candy Cream." The way Sierra said it, it sounded like she was proud of it.

So he grinned and said, "That's a great name. You came up with that yourself?"

"Sure did."

She had melted some toward him, and he liked that, tried not to let it make him nervous, like he had to keep impressing her in order to get her to keep talking to him.

He thought the bikes were a win, anyway.

"So I take it the candy shop is maybe going to have ice cream too?"

"Yeah. And you figured it out by the name." Sierra's smile was smug.

He grinned back at her. "I sure did."

"I thought so. It is a good name. Someone just looking at the sign should be able to figure out that they can get candy and ice cream in there."

"Yeah. Kind of like free advertising."

"Yep." She snapped her seatbelt on as he put the truck in gear, and they started to pull out. "Mom said I can work the counter, and she might be helping the lady across the street, whose kid is dying from cancer. I haven't actually seen that lady yet."

"Really?" A pang hit his heart. It could be his kid. And he'd feel even guiltier for not spending time with her like he should have. "That's sad."

"I know. Everybody's been pitching in so that they can keep the diner open and she can take care of her kid." Sierra shrugged, looking out the window. "Apparently, her husband ditched her."

"I see." He wasn't really tempted to say "the way your mother ditched me," but the thought went through his head. It wasn't the same. Lindy didn't ditch him.

# Chapter 16

SIERRA AND ADAM HAD a good time riding bikes and eating their sandwiches on the beach. He felt good about their relationship by the time they were done, happy that he'd been able to get her to laugh.

The ride home didn't feel stilted at all, and they talked pretty easily, with only a couple of silences that didn't even feel awkward.

They pulled in beside Lindy's car, and Lindy came out on the porch.

Before the pickup was completely shut off, he said to Sierra, "Thanks for going with me today. I had a great time."

"Thanks for spending time with me, Dad. I appreciate it," Sierra said, a little flippantly, as she grabbed her door handle and opened the door, hopping out.

He supposed it was pretty sad when his own daughter had to thank him for spending time with her.

He couldn't do anything about the past, but he felt like he'd started building a pretty solid foundation for the future today.

He hoped he could do that with his wife, although he had a feeling it wasn't going to be nearly as easy.

Getting out of his truck and opening up the door to the back of the cab, he grabbed the box that he picked up at the post office. He closed the door and walked to the porch where Lindy stood, talking to Sierra.

"All right," Lindy said to Sierra as he came closer. "Can we talk more about it in a minute? I'll be in."

"Sure, Mom." Sierra looked over her shoulder at her dad. "Thanks a lot, Dad. I had a really great time."

"You're welcome. Anytime." And he meant that.

He lifted a hand, and she waved her clarinet case before awkwardly grabbing the door and walking inside.

"Looks like that was pretty easy for you," Lindy said, and he detected more than a little bitterness in her voice. He deserved it.

"I wouldn't say easy. But yeah. She forgave me faster than I deserve, that's for sure." He searched her eyes, looking for a sign of softness. He didn't see any. In fact, she almost seemed angry. "It was a start. I hope it was a start to a much better relationship than what I've had with her. I intend to put all the effort I can into it."

Her lip pulled back and her brows jerked, almost as though she were saying "yeah, right."

But she didn't say anything aloud, and she seemed to deliberately try to soften her stance, almost as though she knew she was being defensive and angry.

"Thanks. It was nice of you to make the effort." Her tone didn't quite match her words, but he viewed it as a good sign that she was trying.

"I'm sorry that you feel like you have to thank me for spending time with my daughter."

That made her eyes snap to his. If there was any hardness left on her face, it eased out.

"Me too."

"Thanks for letting me."

"Of course. You're her dad. I'm glad you want to."

He thought that was true. It probably didn't make her happy that Sierra seemed so easy. He wasn't completely sure that Sierra was totally okay with him, but he supposed he owed Lindy more.

"I think one of the reasons that Sierra isn't angry at me is because you haven't been talking about me."

Lindy's face moved a little, but she didn't say anything.

"I appreciate that. It wouldn't have been hard for you to turn her against me. I can't say I don't deserve that."

Both lips pulled in, and he thought she was trying not to cry. Maybe she was thinking about times where she'd covered for him. She must have. He knew he missed birthdays. He'd never miss Christmas, but he hadn't done any shopping. Lindy always took care of the gifts and the wrapping and decorations and the cookies and lights, and all he did was show up.

He couldn't say any of that though. Where would he start?

Not now anyway.

Suddenly remembering he was holding a box in his hand, he held it out to her. "I'm sorry." He looked over at the tent where he'd been staying. "I don't have any wrapping paper."

A moment before, he'd been afraid she was going to cry; now, the corners of her lips were twitching up.

"I see. Maybe you'll have to get some."

"Yeah. I'll build a shelf in there specifically for wrapping paper. Maybe I'll need it."

He was thinking this wasn't the last of the gifts he intended to give Lindy. Not that he thought that he could buy her affections, but he'd noticed while packing up his house that she hadn't seemed to take any of the candles she always had sitting around, so he'd ordered one to the P.O. box he set up in Blueberry Beach. He'd just gotten the delivery notification this morning.

"I thought you might like one of these." He shook the box a little, because she hadn't reached for it.

"You don't have to give me gifts."

"I know. That wasn't the problem. But let me, please?"

Her lips tightened down, but she took the box.

"Goodness. I'm not going to be able to open this." She pulled at the tabs, which were taped down with shipping tape nice and tight.

He reached into his pocket and pulled out his knife.

"Here. Let me."

Three swipes, and he had all the tape cut. It took a little bit, and he gave her a hand pulling open the box, but she eventually pulled out the pretty candle he'd bought for her.

She smiled, holding it up. "It's my favorite scent too. Was that an accident?"

"I'm not sure you're supposed to be looking a gift horse in the mouth." He had to tease her a little and was rewarded with a little twinkle in her eye. "But no. It's the scent that I love the best too."

"Oh," she said, like that said everything. It probably did, remembering what Pastor Rendell had said about him being selfish. "I'm sorry," she said, sounding sincere. "That was rude. Thank you. I do appreciate it. There aren't any candle shops around, and I didn't bring any with me."

"About that. Everything from the house is in storage. Furniture, papers, books, everything."

"Thank you. I wondered. Mostly about my mother's china and some other dishes and stuff." She hesitated. "The kitchen table."

He'd known it meant a lot to her. "All in storage. I hired people to come in and pack it, because I knew I wouldn't be able to do it without breaking a bunch of stuff. Hopefully, they were able to. I really don't know what kind of condition it's in, though."

"That's fine. I appreciate you making the effort."

"Yeah, well, I knew I was selling the house without saying anything to you, and as much as I wanted to, I also needed to get it done and get out here."

"I see." Maybe she did. He hoped so. That she heard some of the desperation he had, and understood. He wanted her to.

"Well, thanks for the candle." It sounded like a dismissal, but she didn't turn to go.

"Someone said you own a store?" He meant it as a statement, but it came out as a question.

Maybe he wanted to see it, but it seemed like guilt flashed across her face.

"I guess I don't blame you for not telling me about it. But if you want to talk about it sometime, I'd love to hear about it."

"It's opening Saturday. Sierra named it."

"Yeah. She told me. Blueberry Candy Cream. A candy and ice-cream store."

She turned the jar in her hand. "Maybe we should have candles too."

"I think that's a good idea. You would have had a customer in me today."

That made her smile, and he felt a little surge of victory go through him.

"I'll have to think about that. I know I can do the candy, but the ice cream is new, and I'll have to figure out managing that. Although the previous owner had it."

"So you bought it already stocked by the previous owner?"

"Yeah. A lot of the stuff was already in there. They didn't quit because they went out of business. She had parents who were ill, and she had to take care of them."

"Nice. So it's a profitable place."

"I believe so. It felt like a good risk anyway. I used money from my savings."

He nodded. He'd known that she had a separate savings account that she used to put the money from her job she had left over. "Maybe I can come to the opening?"

"Of course. I'm not going to bar people from patronizing my store."

"Good to know that I'm not on the do-not-serve list."

"Not yet." She said it with a little bit of a glint in her eye, and he almost thought that she might have been teasing him. Made him feel good, encouraged.

"What time?"

"We're opening at ten, and I'll be giving a free cone to everyone who stops in. You can get one too."

"I was actually thinking about ice-cream cones the other day."

"Really?" Her brows drew down as her hands twisted the lid off the candle, pulling it off and sniffing.

"Really. I was thinking about how when you and I were first dating, we used to get one and share it." He looked at her, watching her face, as her eyes, a little surprised, flew to his.

Maybe they darkened a bit; he felt like his did.

She remembered, he could see it on her face, how sharing an ice-cream cone, of all things, felt extremely romantic.

Seconds ticked by as they looked at each other. Man, he couldn't say for sure what she was feeling, but he certainly wished that they were closer.

Suddenly, she blinked, then turned away.

"Thanks for the candle," she said, facing the door.

"Lindy?"

"Yes?"

"Saturday night, to celebrate your opening, would you be interested in going out with me?"

He wasn't going to ask her so soon. He was going to spend more time getting to know her. Doing things around the house.

She hesitated, and he knew he'd moved too fast.

"If you don't mind, I think I'll probably be tired after the opening, and I'd rather not." She lifted her hand to the doorknob, then paused. "Maybe some other time?"

It wasn't a flat-out no, but it wasn't a very encouraging maybe.

"Do you mean that?"

She hesitated, then she looked down. "I just need some time. Sorry. I really appreciate your efforts."

"No, I understand. You spent a long time being neglected. I didn't think I could just waltz in here and have everything fall in my lap."

She looked disappointed. He hoped it was disappointment in herself. "I'm sorry. I really am. But I think it would probably be wrong of me to say yes when I'm not feeling it."

"Sometimes, we just need to do the right thing before the feeling comes." He was desperate, but he believed it too. He just hoped she didn't think he was lecturing her.

"I know. Just give me some time, please? Let me get through the opening. I've never run a business of my own before."

He nodded. "I know. We shared a little bit."

"Yeah."

She didn't add "before you took it away," but she didn't really need to. He was thinking it himself.

He should never have done that. Maybe the business had grown and expanded more once he'd moved it out of his house, but it had moved him away from his wife, and away from his daughter, and away from what really mattered to him.

"For what it's worth, I regret that."

"Me too."

He didn't ask what she regretted. He knew.

"I'm going to take a walk on the beach, but I'll be in my tent the rest of the evening, if you need me."

"Thanks for letting me know."

"You're welcome."

"Good night."

"Take care."

She gave him a little smile before she turned and walked in the house.

He watched her go until the door shut behind her. He wanted to follow but knew he couldn't. Not yet.

She wouldn't even agree to go out with him yet. He'd given her a gift, spent time with Sierra, both of which he wanted to do, though both were things that maybe he wouldn't have thought of normally.

Maybe he could think of something else. Something not quite as intimidating as a date.

Anything to try to win his wife.

# Chapter 17

LINDY BACKED HER CAR up to the beach house.

She'd gotten a stepladder from the hardware store along with a five-gallon can of paint, a bucket of primer, and a sprayer.

She felt guilty for saying no to Adam last night. She wished she had had the courage to accept.

He seemed to understand. Although, honestly, she wasn't sure she understood herself.

She wanted to go out with him. But...she was afraid to trust, to believe that things had really changed and she wouldn't fall in love all over again, just to sit at home alone and wonder what was wrong with her that her husband didn't want to do anything with her.

She'd managed to scrape one side of the house. The forecast called for rain later this week. She wanted to get it primed at least so the rain didn't soak into the old boards.

She noticed the tent in the yard and felt a pang of guilt.

Her husband shouldn't have to stay in the yard in a tent.

But she hadn't asked him to come, and the loveseat would be uncomfortable for either one of them.

She sighed. Maybe she should just go somewhere else and let him have the house.

Sierra had practice after school, so Lindy had a couple of hours. Tomorrow was the grand opening of Blueberry Candy Cream, and she'd stopped in after dropping Sierra off, just to check the store one more time, but everything was set.

Nothing was scheduled for the rest of the afternoon until she had to pick Sierra up, so it was a good time to start painting.

Popping the trunk, she struggled to get the stepladder out from around the large bucket of primer.

"Can I give you a hand with that?"

Her husband's voice still gave her shivers. She wished it didn't.

She turned and tried to smile. "Thank you." She stepped back, sincerely appreciating that he was helping her.

She realized he was wearing old clothes and looked dusty, like he'd been working.

She wondered where.

And then she saw the scraper sticking out of his back pocket.

She didn't mind painting so much, but scraping was hard work, and she did appreciate him helping.

Not that she'd expected it; it surprised her.

"You just hold on, I'll come back for the bucket of paint. Where do you want this?"

She looked up at him. His eyes looked kind and somewhat sad. Like hers, it was certainly older than when they married.

There were crinkles at his eyes, which were still the deep blue that she remembered.

Maybe his hairline was receding some, and he was slightly heavier set, but it had never mattered to her what he looked like.

Not really.

She supposed she appreciated the fact that he wasn't afraid to take a shower. A bad smell might get annoying, but he'd always been careful to take care of himself, and he'd never complained about her imperfections.

Ever. Not even one time.

She actually kind of liked him exactly the way he was. Like he'd lived life and wasn't a smart-aleck kid anymore.

Not that he was ever a smart aleck. He was always serious and hard-working.

But now he looked down at her, waiting, willing to do what she wanted and asked.

He had never been impatient, either. Some women complained that their husbands were short tempered, but she most definitely couldn't.

She shook her head. "I have the back side of the house ready except for the very top. That's where I was going to start."

"All right, I'll take it back. Is that where you want the paint too?"

"Yes, please."

He grabbed the ladder out of her car, twisting it and pulling it out, taking the time to figure it out where she just got frustrated.

He always had more patience than she did.

With his other hand, he grabbed the bucket of paint.

His eyes met hers, and he paused just a fraction of a second, maybe as though he were going to stop and say something else, but he didn't and he carried them around the back of the house.

She closed the trunk and walked to the back car door, opening it and grabbing the bags of groceries from the seat.

Frustration pulled at the back of her neck.

Frustration that he was here. Frustration that he was in a tent in his own yard. Frustration that she couldn't bring herself to trust him that he wasn't going to go back and do the exact same things that he'd been doing.

He'd been neglecting her for years. It was so hard to think that all the sudden he changed.

But he never just hung around before, waiting for her to pull in so he could carry her things out.

Sighing, she used her hip to shut the car door and walked up the steps and into the house.

When she had the groceries put away, she heard some noises coming from the back of the house and went and looked out the window.

He was on the stepladder, using the scraper to get the last few inches that she had been going to get.

She couldn't paint while he was scraping, so she went back to the kitchen and got started on supper.

Thoughts of her own business ran through her head. She understood it was hard to get started, and there were a lot of things involved, and she had been completely wrapped up in it.

She'd still made sure to spend time with Sierra every day after school, just chatting and being available in case Sierra wanted to talk about something.

She seemed to have gotten involved in school, and her classes were going okay. She'd made friends pretty quickly, too.

The music helped. The fact that there was a sidewalk band, and Sierra was able to join, had gotten her excited about being here, and Lindy almost thought that in a few months, Sierra might be actually happy they'd moved.

Still, it was hard to leave old friends.

Her phone rang while she was waiting for the pasta water to boil, and she saw it was her mom.

Stifling a sigh—she had been kind of busy and hadn't called her mom as much as she should have—she swiped.

"Hello?"

"Lindy. Have you forgotten that you have a mother?"

Lindy closed her eyes and took a big breath. She blew it out.

Opening her eyes, she grabbed the dishrag so she could wipe cupboards. She might as well do something constructive with her frustration while she was on the phone.

"I'm sorry, Mom. It's been kind of busy here. I should have called you, and I didn't."

"Well, I figured I might as well give you a ring and see if you were still alive or not. I guess it's my job to check on you."

"I'm sorry. I'll try to do better. I just got wrapped up in some things. You know how it is with moving everything."

"I do. But I never actually moved away from your father. So I don't know how it is like that."

Lindy scrubbed the cupboard harder and scrunched her mouth up, thankful it wasn't a FaceTime call, because whatever her mouth was doing couldn't be considered a smile in any language.

"I know, Mom. You're right. I...I don't know if I'm doing the right thing."

"You obviously are not. Your place is with your husband."

"I know." She put her phone on speaker and set it on the counter. That way, she could use both hands, one to anchor herself and the other to scrub the dirt and possibly the paint off the cupboard doors. "I know what I did probably wasn't right. But I also know that it was necessary."

"In your opinion. There's no reason why you couldn't just stay there. The next thing you'll be doing is filing for divorce."

"I'm not gonna do that, Mom. And I'm not fighting with him, and...he's here." She almost hadn't told her mom that.

She didn't know what it meant, and she figured her mom would probably forgive him immediately and expect her to, too. It wasn't that she wasn't forgiving him, it's just that she...didn't feel like she could trust him.

"What? He's there?" Her mom tsk-tsked. "Well, he's taking you back, obviously. You better go."

"Actually, no. He...he sold the business and our house."

"He sold your house?"

Her parents lived in Erie, having moved there when her dad got transferred from Latrobe where she'd grown up to the northern part of the state. She loved visiting them, loved the beautiful sandy beaches of

Lake Erie, which was surely part of the reason why she loved the beach house here in Lake Michigan so much.

Lake Erie just seemed smaller, and a little bit tamer, than Lake Michigan. There probably wasn't any difference; it's just the way she felt when she saw them.

"He did. Apparently, it sold quickly."

"Where did you move? What did he do with everything? What about my china?"

"He said he put everything in storage. And he...moved out here."

"That's great. I'm so glad you finally came to your senses. I do think that you were very much in the wrong for doing what you did, but it sounds like it all worked out."

"Yeah. I guess it did." There was no way in the world that she was going to tell her mom that her husband was camping out in the yard in the tent.

No way.

Her mom would insist she should just give up her bed and offer to go out to the tent.

Maybe she really would do that. Then she would stop feeling guilty.

"Your father and I are coming out to visit. Sometime."

Lindy didn't try to talk her out of it as much as she might want to. Knowing her luck, her mom would suspect something was wrong and leave today.

"Give me a heads-up, because there's not much room at the beach house. You know that."

"We would probably stay at the hotel we stayed at before and just come to your house during the day."

"Sure. Sounds great, Mom. Although maybe you should give me a little bit of notice, because...because I...I...I'm opening a candy and ice-cream shop on Main Street, right by the lake." The last lines came out in a rush. This was going to send her mom to the moon.

"You did what? You opened a business? What about your husband? Isn't he opening it with you? Aren't you doing this together? Isn't that why he sold his business? And, wait! A candy store? Lindy. There's no future in a candy store."

Yeah. That's kind of what she thought was going to happen. Actually, that was a lot tamer than what she thought might happen.

"I thought it would be fun."

"Life is not about what is 'fun.'" Her mother spit that word out like it had four letters. "You have to be responsible. And you have to be...professional. A candy store? I mean anyone can open a candy store. Why don't you do something that I can be proud of with your life?"

Lindy rinsed the rag off in the sink and wrung it out with both hands, biting her lip.

She supposed, if any of her friends were listening to her mom, they'd be horrified at some of the things she said.

Her mom was certainly entitled to her opinion, and Lindy hoped that when she made sense, Lindy listened to her.

And was respectful when she didn't.

But...but she wasn't after the prestige of a big job. She didn't care about that. That wasn't what made her happy and never had.

Her mom wouldn't understand, but she seemed to be waiting for Lindy to say something, so Lindy tried one more time to explain it to her mom.

"You know how you volunteer to chair the charity gala every year?"

"That has nothing to do with this."

"And how for years you used to run the foreign student exchange program?"

"I don't understand what you're saying."

"I'm just saying you did those things because they made you happy, right?"

"It had nothing to do with making me happy." She said "happy" like it had germs.

"Doing those things made you feel fulfilled. Like you were giving back. Like you were doing what God wanted you to do in your life."

"Well, certainly. Of course, God wants me to do those things, and that's exactly why I did them. That's why I recycle. That's why I don't use plastic. Because it makes me feel good about my contribution to the world." Her mother cleared her throat. "That has nothing to do with your job. Which is a mark of prestige. It's what you do to earn a living, and there are certain jobs that are prestigious, and jobs you can take pride in, and jobs where other people look at you and say that's great. You have a great job. And there's a future where you can work toward things."

Her mother's voice got the tone that she always used when she talked to Lindy. The one where she treated her like she was a little girl. "That's not what a candy store owner does. Owning a candy store is not a prestigious job. It's like a little kid thing. Lindy, you have so much potential. You could do so much with your life. Why do you refuse to see that?"

She didn't think her mom would understand. She never had before when she tried to explain it to her.

Still, she couldn't stop herself.

"I don't want to have the stress of a high-powered job. I just want to relax and have fun with my life. I want to enjoy the people around me. I want to be able to be a blessing to them, and if I'm constantly stressed about my job, constantly working to make sure that everything is perfect, and making sure that I'm getting properly ahead, I can't smile, and sip tea while I watch the sun rise, and then sit with my friends, and wait tables for a lady whose son is dying of cancer while I put my arm around someone else as we cry on each other's shoulders. Mom, that's what I want. I just want my life to make a difference. And it doesn't have to make a difference on a global scale. I just want my life to make a difference right here in Blueberry Beach."

"Fine. You can do what I did. Your life can make a difference wherever you are while you volunteer to do whatever it is that you were saying you want to do, and at the same time, you can have a good job. A job where you actually make money. A job that supports your husband and goes where he goes. A job where people don't look at you and scratch their head and wonder why you're content with being in a dead end."

"Right, Mom. I'm sure you're probably right." Lindy's voice was subdued.

It wasn't that she was giving up, and honestly, she'd had this conversation with her mom so many times that it really didn't even bother her anymore. She and her mom would never agree on it. And her mom gave her a hard time with it because that's what moms did, because she loved Lindy. And Lindy would listen to it, and she'd go on and keep doing what she knew she was created to do.

She knew very few people who actually had parents who were extremely happy and satisfied with what their kids did anyway.

Most of the time, people's parents were trying to get them to do something else. Why would hers be any different?

"So tell Daddy I said hi, okay?" she said, picturing her dad reading the newspaper in his recliner and peeking over it as her mother called over, "Lindy says hi, Fred."

She heard her dad murmuring in the background, and her mom said, "He said to tell you to be a good girl and don't forget to lock your door."

"Tell him I won't."

She didn't even know where the key for the door was. She hadn't locked it when she left, and she probably wasn't going to start.

No point in telling her parents that.

She had four cupboard doors scrubbed, and the backstop to the counter, by the time she finally hung up with her mom.

The water had boiled, and she'd put the lasagna noodles in as well.

Talking to her mom always made her feel slightly disquieted. Not upset necessarily, just because she accepted that they were different, but a restless feeling like she needed to reexamine everything and make sure that she wasn't missing something.

Sometimes, she was so sure of herself. So sure she was right she didn't take the time to question whether or not she might be blind.

So many people never thought to question what they were doing, just did what they always did or did what they thought they knew was the right thing, and yet, if they would just think about it, they'd realize it wasn't.

She thought of Adam.

Going along, trying as hard as he could to make his business successful, certain he was doing the right thing. But maybe he really did see now that he could have been making better decisions.

Was she like that too?

Taking the wooden spoon, she stirred the lasagna noodles, turning them down.

The scraping against the house had stopped, and she walked back to look out the window.

Adam had gotten the top scraped, apparently, and was now working on the sprayer that she had bought earlier. He already had the lid off the paint.

She went over to the sliding glass door and debated for all of three seconds before she opened it and walked down to the porch, leaning around the side of the house.

"You don't have to do that."

He stopped what he was doing and looked up, startled. "Sneaking up on me?"

"Just wanted to see if I could scare you."

"You did, actually."

"Deep in thought, huh?"

"I guess. This has needed to be done for years." He jerked his head at the house and then the painting he was doing.

"I know. It's a big job."

"Yeah. I figured I'd help you. I heard that it was supposed to rain tomorrow. You've got this all scraped, I hate to see it get wet."

"That was my thought. That's why I got the stepladder and the primer."

"I figured. But I don't like to see you work too hard," he said, and there was a gentle tilt in his voice, like he really did care.

She supposed the question of whether or not he cared should never come up. But it just felt like when he never spent any time with her, never talked to her, never asked about her...sure. Any normal, rational person would have wondered if he really cared.

Now, obviously, he did, but for how long?

"It's work I enjoy. You know that," she finally said.

"Do you mind that I'm doing it?"

"No. I wanted to ask if you wanted to come in when it's time for supper. Feeding you is the least I can do since you're doing this."

He stopped, his hands freezing, before he looked up slowly. "Don't feel like you have to."

She didn't. She really didn't. She was grateful that he was doing it, but...she supposed she was asking him because he was doing something nice for her, and she felt bad. But she didn't feel like she had to.

"I don't. I'm making lasagna. I just know you love it."

His mouth curved up in a slow grin. Man, back in the day, that could really send her heart into conniptions. Actually, her heart was kind of doing the conniption thing now.

"No one makes lasagna like you."

"We're having it for supper, and I'm making enough for three. If you'd like to come."

"You know I'll be there. Five?"

"It'll be a little bit after, because I pick Sierra up at five. Maybe 5:30?"

"That's perfect. When you leave to get her, I'll quit and go in and take a shower."

She nodded, not feeling entirely comfortable with him. Awkward, but awkward in a kind of exciting way. Which was odd.

"I'll set a place for you."

"Thanks."

"Of course."

"It's not of course, and we know it."

She just had a conversation with her mom, and she really didn't want to have another hard, emotional, frustrating conversation. So she jerked her chin and turned, walking back into the house and finishing the lasagna.

Part of her was dreading tonight. She wanted to put this part of her life behind her and build something new so she wasn't constantly feeling like she wasn't worth anything because her husband obviously didn't care about her, didn't want her, and didn't want to spend time with her.

But on the other hand, she was kind of excited. After all, she hadn't left because she didn't love him anymore. And she hadn't left because he couldn't still make her heart race.

And she just couldn't get rid of the thought that maybe there was a chance for them after all.

# Chapter 18

ADAM FINISHED HIS SHOWER, stepping out and toweling off, excited about the evening.

Lindy hadn't even seemed upset. When he suggested she might be asking him for dinner out of guilt or feeling like she had to, she'd been sincere when she said she wasn't.

Lindy didn't lie. Of course, he didn't believe she was perfect or anything, but he knew she wouldn't lie. If she hadn't wanted him to eat with them, she wouldn't have asked.

Of course, he wasn't sure *why* she'd asked.

Maybe he didn't want to know. He didn't think she'd up and decided because he'd scraped some paint off, and sprayed for her, that she'd changed her mind and everything was okay.

Plus, he'd definitely noticed that she hadn't said he could move back in.

But progress. He was hopeful.

He'd cleaned up his painting equipment and showered, and they still weren't back.

He checked his watch. Five twenty.

He wondered if she was talking to that man. Gage. Who seemed like a man he might actually like if he wasn't concerned his wife had a thing for him.

He couldn't torture himself with thoughts like that.

He had the opportunity to eat with her. What was he going to say? What should he do?

116

She'd given him an invitation, but after racking his brain, he couldn't think of anything else he could do.

Checking the drive again, he decided maybe he had a little time and he would call Pastor Rendell to see if he had any advice.

Pulling his phone out, he brought up his contacts and clicked on the pastor.

The phone rang twice before Pastor Rendell answered.

"Hello?"

"You know I didn't realize until just now that you might be eating supper. Am I interrupting you?"

"No. Actually, I'm on my way home. But I can talk for a few minutes."

"Nothing important. I just...I'm out here in Michigan, like I told you I was going to be, and she's talking to me. And I followed your advice and bought a tent to set up in the yard, so as not to push her or make her feel like I was demanding reconciliation...."

He paced, noticing that the table had been set neatly, with a vase and flowers in the middle.

His eyes hooked on it, and he stared. The little details that Lindy did that he wouldn't even think of, and yet when she was gone, everything looked barren. Spartan. And that was why. Because her little touches weren't there.

"So how are things going?" Pastor Rendell asked when Adam didn't say anything.

"Well. I had the opportunity to carry some things for her, a paint bucket and stepladder, and then I just went ahead and did the scraping that she was going to do. And I ended up painting that side of the cottage. Then, she invited me for supper."

"Sounds good. You're sure she didn't feel like she had to?"

"No. I asked. And Lindy doesn't lie. I'm sure she meant it when she said she wanted to."

"That's progress."

"That's what I thought. But, okay, I know I have a little trouble admitting this, but I'm nervous. I don't know what to do. And I don't want to miss this opportunity. Any ideas?"

He hated sounding like such a nervous wreck. Normally, he was very confident in his business transactions. In fact, there wasn't a single business transaction that he'd ever done where he'd been this nervous.

Pastor Rendell was silent for a while, and Adam figured if they were sitting in his office, he'd have his fingers steepled together, tapping the first fingers together and thinking.

Finally, he said, "I think you just need to keep on the way you are. Look for opportunities to do things. What's her love language?"

"Love language?"

"Does she like gifts?"

"I...guess. I got her a candle, and she seemed to like it."

The pastor sighed. "Well, I'll email you a book link, and in the meantime, you can just hit them all. What you did today was an act of service. Tonight is spending time with her. Maybe you could compliment her or something. That would be words. And if you see something she enjoys...something small so she doesn't feel overwhelmed. The candle is a good start. Does she have a favorite candy bar? A favorite soda? Does she like flowers? Maybe there's something else that she likes? Could you pick up a small gift for her?"

Pastor Rendell had been throwing questions at him so quickly he hadn't had a chance to answer. But his mind was whirling.

He didn't recall that she really liked flowers, although she did have some on the table. And she didn't drink soda. But she did have a favorite candy bar. And...he seemed to recall at their house there was almost always something out on the table.

Maybe he could get her something like that.

"You could also see, if she seems receptive, maybe she'd be interested in a walk. Although..." Pastor Rendell hesitated. "I don't think I would ask her tonight. It might be too soon. But you could definitely think about something simple. Maybe you could sit on the porch together. Watch the sunset. Or the sunrise. Grab her a coffee. Ask her to go for a bicycle ride with you, or maybe the whole family could do something."

"But not tonight."

"No. I would not push any more tonight. Did you finish with the stuff outside?"

"No. The rest of the house needs to be done. But I was already gonna do that."

"Good. I would. And don't do these things just to get her back. I think she'll be able to see that. You want to do them because you love her and you enjoy making her happy. Do you understand what I'm saying?"

Adam paused in his pacing, rubbing his eyes before taking his hand down and staring at the wall. He knew exactly what Pastor Rendell was saying. Basically, he could be doing these things as a means to an end. Just trying to get her back, because that's what he wanted. He wanted his wife with him.

Or he could do those things, not expecting anything from her in return. Kind of the way he did with the stepladder and the paint. He had just seen his wife struggling to get something out of the trunk of her car and had come over to help her. He hadn't thought of doing it for her to get credit or for her to give him something back.

"You want to give freely. With no expectations," Pastor Rendell finally said when Adam didn't reply. "That's what love is. Love is giving, with no expectations of getting anything in return. In fact, that's really the way it should be in your marriage all the time. You're just looking for things to do or to say or to just be with her, whatever it is that makes her happy. Because you want her to be happy. Not because you have to or because you want something."

"I see. I understand. It's not about bribing or ulterior motives."

"Exactly. No ulterior motives. It's just for the enjoyment of being a blessing to someone you love no matter what they do to you. Remember we talked about love being less of a feeling and more about a deliberate choice followed by actions that back up that choice?"

"Yes. That makes sense." It wasn't a totally new way of thinking. But it wasn't the kind of thinking that came naturally.

"And don't forget about Sierra. I'm not saying this as a shortcut, but a lot of times, women especially love to see people being kind to their children. It's a blessing to them and makes them appreciate the person who's doing the kindness. You might want to try it. But, again, because you love your daughter and want to spend time with her, not because you're trying to get something from your wife. Understand?"

"Yeah. I see that she does those kinds of things for me all the time. Or that she used to. I guess that's why she invited me to supper and is making my favorite."

"Your favorite?"

"Yeah. But I don't think that she knew that I was going to be here or that she was going to see me. I don't know. She used to make my favorite all the time, even if I was late and she had to hold it for me."

"Well, good. Let me know how it goes. I'm pulling into my driveway."

"I appreciate it, pastor."

"Not a problem."

They hung up.

Adam felt better, although he wished, since everything seemed so simple, that he could have figured it out for himself.

Why did he need someone else to tell him that he should be looking for ways to make his wife happy? Doing things that made her smile?

Isn't that something he did naturally back when they were dating? Even when they were first married, he just looked for ways to be kind and to make her laugh.

Pastor Rendell hadn't said anything about that, but he felt like when they laughed together, there was some kind of bonding that went on. Maybe it was just his imagination.

Still, maybe he could make a short trip into town and pick up a few things that might let her know that he was thinking about her.

He couldn't overwhelm her, though. He had a tendency to want to just pour out on her, and Pastor Rendell had warned him pretty strongly about that.

He saw her car coming up over the rise, and he went to the door, walking out.

Shoving his phone in his pocket, he waited for them to park with his hands in his pockets and his shoulder against the porch post.

If she had anything to carry, he would carry it for her, but he supposed walking down and opening her door might be a little bit much.

He was still tempted to.

Sierra kind of eyed him, standing there on the porch, like she wasn't too sure what he was doing there, which of course made him feel bad.

His child shouldn't wonder what her dad was doing at their house. Even if they were in Pennsylvania, it would be a really odd occurrence for her to see her dad just standing on the porch, waiting for them to come home, and not with the phone in his hand or the computer opened in front of him, if he even was home before they were. Which was hardly ever.

"Sierra, I'm sorry. I forgot to tell you that I invited your father to eat with us tonight," Lindy said as she closed her car door and slung her purse over her shoulder. He wondered if she'd forgotten on purpose because it was just too weird to have "invited" her dad to eat.

"Oh. Okay." Sierra cracked her gum, shoved her big book bag over her shoulder, and carried her instrument case in her free hand as she used her knee to shut her door.

Lindy reached the porch steps first and started up them. He opened the screen door and held it for her after turning the knob on the other door and pushing it open.

"Thank you," she said as she walked in.

He held the door for Sierra, and she gave him an eyeball as she walked in.

He walked in as well, closing the door behind him and feeling a little awkward. He wasn't used to feeling like a stranger in his own home, and he wasn't used to not doing anything.

Sierra had gone straight back to her room while Lindy had put her purse away and gone to the sink to wash her hands.

She was drying them as he said, "Is there something I can do to get supper on the table?"

She turned around, her brows raised.

It had been a long time, if ever, that he'd helped with supper.

Pastor Rendell hadn't exactly said, but maybe just working together was another thing that was good for them. Being in each other's presence and handing things off. Just something fun about that.

Or relationship building. Maybe that was a man thing. Maybe women built relationships by talking, and men built relationships by doing. Or maybe he was just an idiot. He didn't know.

Regardless, she hung the towel up very carefully, deliberately almost, and said, without looking at him, "I have the lasagna sitting on the stove. You can carry it to the table. I have the bread warming in the oven and a salad in the refrigerator. Once I pour everyone a glass of water, we'll be ready."

He took two steps forward while she turned and walked toward the stove as well. They stopped, a little catty-corner from each other.

"I...thought you want me to get the lasagna?"

"Yes. Go ahead. I'll wait to get the bread out."

Maybe if he were a teenager, he would have taken the opportunity to bump into her or at least brush against her. But considering his age, he thought that maybe he ought not. Still, the idea was tempting. It was hard to be around her this way and not want to touch her.

Pastor Rendell had not said anything about touching his wife. He supposed Pastor Rendell had considered him intelligent enough to know that it probably wasn't a good idea.

Although, she did seem to like to hold his hand, or loved to have his arm around her, or enjoyed it when they snuggled together at night. She'd always been a snuggler.

And yet, when he got in bed, long after she had, he'd never snuggled. He hadn't wanted to wake her up, thinking he was being considerate.

Maybe it hadn't been considerate since he was keeping her from doing something she enjoyed.

# Chapter 19

LINDY CARRIED THE WATER pitcher to the table and filled up their glasses.

She thought she was going to have to call Sierra, but she came out of her room, just as she filled the last glass.

Adam's presence hovering, right at the edge of the table, was unfamiliar and made her nervous.

Maybe not necessarily exactly in a bad way, but she was very aware of him.

He hardly ever helped set dinner on the table, and it had been a very long time since they'd all eaten together anyway.

She had two plates at the heads of the table and one alongside.

Sierra sat down immediately at the one alongside as Lindy set the water pitcher down and breathed a sigh of relief.

She wouldn't have to sit beside him.

Not that she didn't want to, it was just... She wasn't sure. She wanted to, but she didn't. And it didn't make sense. She hated these conflicting feelings.

He waited for her to sit down; she almost thought he was going to pull her chair for her, but maybe he was just waiting for her to pick her own chair. She didn't know. She hated this awkwardness that she shouldn't feel around someone she'd been married to for two decades.

He sat down at the head of the table, and their eyes met along its length.

Seconds ticked by between them, and normally, back when they ate together, this was where he would pray.

He seemed to be waiting for some sign from her. Permission maybe?

She wasn't giving it.

They made decisions together, of course, household ones anyway, except the ones he'd abdicated to her. She wasn't going to make this one. He was the head of the household. She'd given him the privilege. He could pray. And she wasn't going to tell him so.

Maybe she was being stubborn, which was odd since she normally wasn't. But she didn't say anything.

Eventually, his face twitched. She wasn't sure whether it was sadness, or maybe humor, or maybe resignation.

But he looked at Sierra, and then he said, "Let's pray."

That part was simple, and she listened quietly with only half an ear, wondering what, if anything, had just happened.

She felt like there was some kind of silent communication passing between them. Maybe a battle almost, but she didn't feel like she'd won.

Not that she had to, it just felt odd.

Still, she loved seeing him at the head of the table. Where he belonged.

Back when they used to eat together, she sat beside him, and it's where she preferred to be. What was the point of being married if they sat with the table between them?

What was the point in being married if they never spent any time together? What was the point of being married if she didn't have anyone to snuggle up to at night?

Rhetorical questions. Ones that didn't really matter anyway.

Except, since he was back, somehow they did.

The first moments of the meal passed in what she felt was awkward silence.

If Adam felt awkward, it didn't show on his face.

Sierra didn't seem to feel anything. If she was happy to see her parents sitting at the same table with her, she didn't look it.

"Do you have any homework tonight?" Adam asked Sierra.

Her head jerked up, her mouth full of lasagna. Her eyes went to her dad and then back to her mom. The expression on her face clearly said, "when did he start caring about whether or not I do my homework?"

Lindy lifted her brows, just a fraction, in a bit of a warning. That wasn't an appropriate question. Sierra had never been allowed to be disrespectful to either one of her parents.

Lindy silently breathed a prayer of thanks that she had never talked badly about her husband to her child. She hadn't excused his behavior, especially whenever Sierra would cry and say "why didn't Daddy come to my recital?" Or "why isn't Daddy here to tuck me in?" Or "why haven't I seen Daddy in a week?" She hadn't done that in recent years. Lindy might not have excused him, but she never said anything bad.

Sierra kinda puffed out a little tiny breath, almost as though saying, "whatever," and looked at her dad. "I do. I have some math I've been trying to catch up on. They're a little ahead of my last school. But I've already learned stuff we're learning in science, so I'm good there."

He nodded, his eyes looking at his daughter, before she looked back down at her plate, and he looked across the table at Lindy.

She kept her face carefully bland and didn't allow anything that she'd been thinking to show.

Was he for real? Did he really care now? Had he always cared and just hadn't been around to ask?

"I heard we're supposed to get some rain tomorrow?" he said, not directing his question at either one of them in particular.

When Sierra didn't say anything, Lindy supposed it was her job to answer. She wanted to talk about something more substantial than the weather.

"I heard that as well."

"I always enjoyed watching it rain here on the beach. Especially when the weather comes from the west."

"I agree. We can watch the rain clouds cross the lake and come up the beach until they finally reach us. It's fun."

He nodded, maybe remembering the one evening they'd done that. They hadn't spent a lot of time together, but they had taken vacations here.

Of course, she'd been here by herself, too. When he'd been too busy to come.

"Have you heard from your parents?" Apparently, he remembered that her mom and she talked at least once a week.

"Actually, I talked with my mom today. I've been kind of lax about calling her, and she called me."

His brows raised. "Someone was in trouble."

The way he said it made her smile. She didn't smile very big. "You're right. I was. For more than just not calling her." She wasn't going to talk about how her mother was on his side. She didn't need both of them ganging up against her. "Mom said that they were going to come see us soon. She didn't say when, and I asked for a little lead time. I'm not sure we'll get it."

He nodded. He knew how her mother was. She hadn't changed since they'd gotten married. Rather pushy and used to getting her way. But not unkind, and she loved them. She wanted the best for them.

"Is your dad well?"

"I imagine so. Mom didn't tell me that he wasn't, and I'm sure I would have heard about it, first thing, if there'd been something wrong."

"I'm sure."

They went back to eating, taking a few more bites in silence.

At least the conversation felt a little bit natural. Not fun, not funny, not flirty at all.

She couldn't remember the last time they'd had a fun, flirty conversation that she enjoyed.

They used to talk for long hours together, about everything.

She almost snorted. Thankfully, she got that stuffed back in time.

Not for years. Years and years and years.

But tonight, he talked about the new hospital, and how they were adding to it, and mentioned Beverly the benefactress.

She didn't mention that she knew Beverly and actually spent time with her in the diner.

From there, the conversation went on in starts and stops, about perfectly neutral topics.

When Sierra was finished eating, she waited for them to finish eating as well and then asked, "May I please be excused?"

"You may," Lindy said, not even waiting for Adam to answer out of habit more than anything. She'd been the one to excuse Lindy and to teach her to wait until everyone was done eating and then take her plate with her and clear the table.

Lindy didn't mind taking care of the rest, as long as Sierra did a little.

"I'm gonna take a shower, then I'm gonna get my homework out," Sierra said as she walked by.

"Okay, thank you."

Sierra walked back to her room.

Lindy pushed back, feeling awkward sitting at the table with just her and Adam. What was she going to say to him?

"Thanks for supper. It was delicious as always."

As it always used to be. It'd been a long time since he'd eaten her cooking when it was good and hot from the oven.

"Thank you." She carried her drink to the kitchen and started taking care of the dishes.

He came out and started helping her. Her traitorous heart beat hard in her chest, and not completely because she was frustrated, more because she liked this new man.

It really did feel like he was a new man. She enjoyed having help with the dishes, and someone to talk to at dinner, and someone to ask their daughter whether or not she was doing her homework and if she had any.

The burden wasn't all hers. It felt good.

But one night didn't erase years.

But it didn't hurt anything, either. They finished up the dishes, and she dried her hands on the tea towel, carefully putting it back, folding it perfectly.

"I guess, I'm, um, gonna go over to my tent."

She took a breath and turned. Facing him. "Would you like me to stay there instead?" she asked with her chin up.

His lips pursed, and his eyes opened wide. "You? With me?"

"No. I just... I don't want to..." She was stuttering. She had the words in her head and forced them out her lips. "I don't want to be the only one that's comfortable," she managed to say. "I'm offering to sleep in the tent, and you can sleep in our bed." Doggone it. She should have said *the* bed. Not *our* bed.

It felt too intimate, and it made his eyes flicker.

Maybe one side of his lip twitched.

"No. I'll stay out."

"Okay." She wasn't gonna argue. She definitely wasn't going to talk about it anymore. She didn't want him to get the very wrong idea that she wanted him to share a bed with her.

Very wrong.

"Thanks again for supper, Lindy."

She swallowed. "You're welcome."

He turned, walking out, closing the door softly behind him.

She watched him stand on the porch for a minute, his hands in his pockets, his eyes on the lake or the horizon. Maybe thinking about the sunset or something else entirely. She had no idea.

She heard Sierra in the hall, and she figured she needed to pull herself together and try to act normal for the rest of the evening. Not let

Sierra see that she wasn't quite sure what she thought about her husband anymore.

# Chapter 20

THE NEXT DAY WAS OVERCAST, but the promised rain hadn't come.

Adam heard Lindy leave while he was on the beach in the early morning, and he assumed she was driving Sierra to school. He hadn't expected her to leave that early and vowed he wouldn't be on the beach the next day when they left.

She didn't come back for hours while he worked around the house, fixing the flower beds that had been sadly neglected.

His stomach growled, announcing lunchtime, but he didn't want to go to town and find out that Lindy was with someone.

He thought last night had gone well. She didn't seem to hate him anyway.

He didn't think there was anyone else, but he didn't want to find out differently.

Plus, he was a little sad and dejected.

Not that he'd expected everything to just fall in place, but he'd expected things to move a little faster, than awkward positions at the dinner table, and even more awkward goodbyes as he walked out the door to his tent in the front yard.

He supposed he deserved this, after the years of neglect, but still.

Remembering what Pastor Randell had said, he decided to take take a break from the flowerbeds, wash up at the hose around the side of the house, and maybe go pick her up something in town.

Not Blueberry Beach, somewhere else.

He decided maybe he could do two nice things for her. He pulled his phone out of his pocket.

**I'm going to town. Do you need anything?**

**No thank you.**

Her answer came back immediately, very prim and proper.

He couldn't remember what her texts were like before.

Before they started just sending the essentials back and forth, like I'll be late for supper. Or Sierra's recital is tonight, did you forget?

He was gone several hours, and when he came home, Lindy's car sat in the drive, and it was almost suppertime.

Pastor Rendell had said not to overwhelm her, but he'd gotten two things, and wanted to give her both.

He'd noticed the card table that they'd always had in the corner of the living room, had been set up, but it was empty.

She almost always had a puzzle on it.

He'd bought her one.

He also had a small bouquet of real flowers, for the vase on the table.

As they'd eaten supper last night, he noticed that the ones that were on the table were fake.

So, the flowers weren't exactly for Lindy. They were for the vase. For the supper table.

He knocked on the door.

Lindy came to the door, an odd expression on her face. Maybe she thought it was awkward answering the door for him. Considering his name was on the deed.

But she didn't say.

"Hello Adam."

"Lindy. I hope you had a good day."

"I did." A little smile tripped around her mouth, and it made him think that she'd had a very good day.

He hoped it hadn't been with someone else.

He stopped that thought.

"I got you something while I was in town today."

"Oh?"

She wasn't inviting him in, so he held up the flowers.

"I noticed last night at the supper table, the flowers you had in the vase and how pretty the table looked.

After you left, all of those little things you used to do to make the room brighter had gone with you. The house looked dark and bare. Last night, I loved the flowers, and I remembered how you use little things to brighten a room. I...I wanted to give you something real to brighten the room with."

He'd practiced that speech the whole way home. Not because he needed to figure out something nice to say, but because he didn't want to stumble over it, and make it sound like he wasn't sincere. Oh, he was *very* sincere.

He wasn't quite sure how to describe the look that passed over her face. Maybe the way a woman might look at a small kitten, or little baby. "Well." She tilted the bouquet. "They're beautiful."

He stood there, waiting.

She pushed the door open, and said, "Supper is ready if you'd like to come in. Gage is dropping Sierra off."

Gage again.

He tried not to allow any look of irritation to cross his face. It wasn't that he didn't like the man, he just didn't like to see the man with his wife.

"I didn't eat all day. I'll accept that invitation if you mean it."

"I do," she said, not immediately, but sincerely.

He stepped in, giving the screen door room to slam behind him.

"I...I brought this for you too. I saw the card table last night and remembered that you always used to have a puzzle out."

She smiled. A real smile as she took the puzzle in her free hand.

"That's a beautiful picture. It looks like it was taken in Yellowstone, maybe."

"I believe you're right. Beautiful flowers, pretty sky." It was the kind of picture he'd noticed she did often.

"The kind I like."

"I thought so. There's lots of sky. That's your favorite to put together."

A memory flashed between them. One of their first dates. Them sitting across from each other at a card table, talking almost nonstop as they put a puzzle together. She worked on the sky, he worked on everything else.

"Thank you," she said, and her voice was slightly softer, maybe just a turn of something else in it. Maybe she was melting toward him. He hoped so.

"Supper smells good."

"Thank you. It's simple. Just chicken and a salad."

"It's more than I'm able to cook in the tent."

She flinched, and he regretted his words. He wasn't trying to make her feel bad. "I'm sorry."

"No, no, no." He held a hand up, although the damage was done. "I didn't mean it like that. I just meant I appreciate that you're cooking supper. And that you invited me."

At the sound of a pickup their heads turned.

"That must be Gage dropping Sierra off."

"I'll go out," he said, not wanting her to.

"All right. I'll finish getting supper on the table. It'll be ready as soon as you guys come in."

"Okay."

He liked that she didn't argue or insist on going out to see Gage. Maybe she'd already seen him all day. Maybe she didn't care. He hoped it was the second.

Gage was his neighbor, and he didn't want to treat him badly, and he didn't dislike him, either.

It wouldn't be a problem if he hadn't neglected his wife to the point he was jealous of every man she looked at.

He walked down the porch stairs and greeted Gage with a comment about the rain that had never come.

Gage said, "We're supposed to get some tonight and according to the forecast, it's going to be heavy."

"Good to know."

"It's pretty cold for camping," Gabe said, indicating the tent in their side yard with his chin.

If Lindy had been with Gage, she had apparently not told him about their living arrangements.

By this time Sierra had climbed out of the truck. From the curiosity on the face of her friend who was sitting on the passenger seat, Sierra hadn't told her what was going on, either.

"I guess something like that." He backed up, raised a hand.

"Thanks for dropping Sierra off. I appreciate it."

"Anytime. Lindy has done enough for me. I owe you."

He wondered exactly what Lindy had done for Gage. Nothing inappropriate he was sure. Lindy wasn't like that.

Of all the problems that he had, that had never been an issue for either one of them.

He'd never even been tempted. Why would he? He had the best wife in the world. He had the woman he loved. "Had" being the operative word there maybe.

Hopefully he could get her back.

Gage lifted his hand in a farewell then wound his window up as he backed out.

Adam went back up the stairs, hoping dinner was slightly less awkward tonight.

# Chapter 21

AT LEAST SUPPER WASN'T quite as awkward as it was the night before. Lindy was grateful for that at least.

Actually, they had all laughed a couple of times. Which was...nice. Made it feel like a real family around the table.

Even when the dark clouds rolled in and it started pouring down rain halfway through their meal, it felt cozy. Her eyes kept landing on the flowers and the vase on the table, and she kept smiling.

Several times she'd done that, only to move her eyes to see Adam staring at her.

It had made her heart flutter. She really thought she was too old to have heart flutters.

She'd certainly been married too long to have them because of her husband. Surely.

But there they were, and she couldn't deny it.

There was something in his gaze, just a serious intensity that almost made her breath catch.

They laughed about several other vacations they'd shared, and how her mom could be over the top.

Sharing those memories and laughing about them had been fun.

Sierra wasn't quite as quick to jump up at the end of the meal, although she did get up before they did, asking to be excused and clearing the table.

Adam and she worked in silence as they scraped the plates and put them in the dishwasher and put the leftovers away.

"If you get hungry tomorrow, they'll be here if you want them," she said, still feeling light and almost...happy.

Not that she wasn't normally happy, she just *felt* happy.

"I'll remember that. Aren't you going to be here?"

"No. There's a lady I'm helping out at the diner tomorrow. I'm going as soon as I drop Sierra off at school."

"I'll be working outside unless you'd like me to meet you?" he asked softly, and not with as much hesitation as he might have had even yesterday.

Her heart turned over.

She could use the help. Normally Dr. Chambers ran the griddle until almost eight o'clock. Typically from eight to ten, it was still very busy, and hard to keep up.

They probably lost business because people didn't get waited on as quickly as they felt they should.

"If you want to. They can always use help."

"Okay. I'll be there."

He hadn't even asked what he'd be doing.

As she dried her hands on the towel, and he walked to the corner to turn and go out the door, he said, "Do you want to drive in with me? I can drop Sierra off at school."

She wasn't sure. If she drove in with him, she was kind of stuck with him all day. Stuck... Was she stuck? Was that the word?

"Maybe we can talk about it in the morning?" she said, which kept her from having to make a decision right now.

"That's fine." He started to turn, then he stopped and said, "Good night."

"Good night," she said.

He turned toward the door and walked out.

Like last night, he stood on the porch for a few minutes, his hand in his pockets, the rain coming down in sheets.

Her heart beat against her spinal cord, each beat making her feel guilty.

It was raining, a cold, Michigan spring rain, and she was sending him to a tent in their yard.

Did it leak?

She'd never met a tent that didn't.

She sighed, her hands clenching and unclenching and clenching again. She needed to act. She needed to move.

She needed to go and ask her husband to stay in the house tonight.

She took in a stabilizing breath, and walked out the door.

He didn't turn right away, just looked over his shoulder, one eyebrow raised in inquiry.

"It's raining," she said. Feeling stupid.

He was standing outside watching it. He knew it.

He didn't make fun of her obviously stupid statement.

He nodded. "Pretty hard."

Rain pounded on the roof, emphasizing the silence between them.

Finally, she opened her mouth and let the words slip out. "You probably ought to stay here tonight."

His brows lifted and his face lit with what could be excitement.

Then he shook his head.

"I know you said that because you have to. Not because you want to. Thank you. But I don't want any 'have to's.'"

It was true. She said because she had to, but his words had made her want to.

"Please? Don't go. Stay in the house. Even if it's just for tonight."

He seemed to think about it, and then he grunted. Turning, he walked to the door, pulling the screen open, but stopping where she stood, with his foot on the step.

"I don't want to be here if you don't want me."

"I don't want you to be in a leaky tent tonight. So tonight, I do want you here. And," she paused, "I'll sleep on the loveseat."

She made that last decision on the spur of the moment, but about half of him would fit on the loveseat, while three quarters of her did. And if she bent her knees, all of her would.

"No. I'll sleep in the loveseat."

"No, I insist. I will sleep in the loveseat. However, if you want clean sheets, You have to make the bed yourself. The sheets are in the second drawer on the right."

He could find the sheets and make the bed. That was her concession.

He nodded his head in agreement. She had spoken in her tone that brokered no arguments. It wasn't one she normally used.

He took a step, then stopped. "Thank you."

She nodded. "I would have felt terrible if you would have refused my invitation and insisted on going out to the tent. So, thank you."

"I may need to use the dryer in the morning, if the tent is leaking like I suspect it is."

"Tents always leak."

They shared a smile. "That's my experience too."

All the experience they had with tents, were experiences they had together.

He stood for a moment like he didn't want to leave her, and she found she wanted him to stay. But she couldn't think of anything to say, and after a few seconds, he walked in the house, heading back to the bedroom and she closed the door against the rain, leaning on it and wondering where she should go from here.

# Chapter 22

LINDY WANTED TO MAKE things right. She wanted to be able to move ahead, but there just felt like a block in her mind where she was afraid to trust.

Afraid that everything would be exactly the way it was before, or just afraid of pain.

Iva May had warned her that she was allowing fear to rule her life, and she didn't want to allow that. She just hadn't figured out how to get over it.

It was still on her mind the next day as she drove in to the diner, Sierra beside her. Sierra was actually going to go and spend some time with Naomi and Lexi, coming down for the ten o'clock opening.

They parted at the diner door, and Lindy waved to Sierra before her daughter crossed the street and went in the door between her candy and ice-cream shop and the surf shop.

Iva May smiled at Lindy as she walked in, the bells jingling over her head. "Today's the day. Are you nervous?"

"A little. I guess I'm more excited than anything. I wonder if I'm up for the challenge. Everything's on me."

"It is. But we'll help. You know everyone will pitch in if you need us to."

"I know." She'd waited enough tables and even cooked a couple of panini sandwiches on the griddle, helping Anitra, whom she'd never met.

Anitra had been spending all of her time at her son's bedside, and from what Lindy had heard, he didn't have much time left.

Dr. Chambers came out to the dining area, carrying a plate with an omelet on it, and set it down in front of a customer, chatting for just a moment at the table.

As he turned, he saw Lindy in the door and threw a hand up. "Today's the day. I'll be there. Everything set?"

"It is. I think. As far as I know." Maybe she *was* nervous. She hadn't thought she was, but she didn't want to fail in front of all these people.

"I'll be there. I sure hope you have ice cream with peanut butter in it."

"We do. I'll save some back for you. I wouldn't want the crowds to get it all before you get there."

"I'm not sure I deserve that special treatment." He grinned, which didn't quite overshadow the sadness that always seemed to lurk in his eyes. "I'll man your counter sometime for free."

"I don't know," she said with a smile. "Just because the doctor can run a griddle doesn't mean that he can run a cash register."

He laughed. "I might need a little help making change, but as long as people pay with cards, I should be good." They shared another laugh together, and he disappeared back in the kitchen.

Iva May already had her coffee made, and she paid for it, saying she was too nervous and excited to eat anything.

"If things stay slow like this, I'll come around and sit down in your parlor a little bit," Iva May said, then she lowered her voice. "If you have a minute, would you go over and sit with Beverly? She seems a little down."

"Thanks. I will." She probably would have done it anyway when she turned and realized Beverly was sitting at the corner table by herself.

Beverly was in her fifties, probably, and of all of the people that hung out in the diner, she was the one that Lindy felt the least comfortable with.

Lindy had heard that she had been the main benefactor of the hospital and was an heiress of some kind or had money somehow, and it made Lindy a little nervous.

Not that Beverly put on airs or was snobbish or anything. She was super nice and really wonderful to talk to.

Lindy always got the feeling that there was a deep regret about her though.

"Good morning," Lindy said, coming over and standing beside the table. "Do you mind if I sit down?"

"No. Please do."

"It's a beautiful morning."

"It is. The summer season will be starting soon. You'll see a lot of sales. Are you ready for your opening?" Her voice was cultured and smooth and sounded younger than what she looked.

"I am. I think." Lindy set her coffee down and sat down on the chair opposite Beverly with a sigh, relishing how good it felt to sit. She had barely even started her day. "I guess there's always things that will probably go wrong, and you can't prepare for everything, but I've done everything I can think of. The next time I have an opening, I'll be more confident."

"You say that as a joke, but you never know. I wasn't expecting to spend my life in business, and look what happened."

"I understand you've done quite well."

"I suppose you could say that," Beverly said, putting a finger on the glass of untouched ice water in front of her.

"Is there something wrong?" Lindy asked when Beverly didn't say anything more.

"Not really. This is just a sad day for me."

"Oh? I'm sorry. Did something happen?" Lindy hadn't heard anything. Surely Iva May would have warned her, but she just said Beverly seemed kind of down.

"Oh no. Not today, specifically. But this would be my daughter's birthday." She smiled sadly at Lindy's surprised expression. "I had a baby. A little girl. She was born alive but died her first night."

"Oh my goodness. I'm so sorry."

"Don't be. It's been a long time, but today would have been her fortieth birthday."

"Oh. That makes today a very sad day."

Lindy didn't know what else to say. And maybe that was why Iva May hadn't come over. She had mentioned her daughter Kim would be turning forty tomorrow. She was coming in for the weekend and might even be in in time for the opening of the ice-cream shop. Maybe Iva May knew that it would make Beverly even more sad to see Kim and be reminded of her own loss.

"Did you grow up in Blueberry Beach?" Lindy knew Iva May had. Interesting that Iva May was so much older than Beverly, and yet they had babies at the same time—children the same age. Or would have, if Beverly's hadn't died.

"I did. My mom's still here. But she doesn't leave the house much. She's never been very social."

"Oh, I see."

Then a new thought struck Lindy. Beverly could not have been very old when she had her baby. If she was fifty-five, which she didn't look, but even if she were closer to sixty, that would still mean she was a teenager when she had her child.

"I was young." Beverly smiled, almost as though she could read Lindy's mind. "Fifteen, in fact."

"Wow."

"Yeah. It was probably for the best." She turned her coffee cup just a little bit, then kind of looked over her shoulder. "Iva May was in the hospital before I was discharged. We were in overnight together. But there was such a spread in our ages that we never really talked."

"That's not such a big difference now, but back then, to a fifteen-year-old, someone who was almost thirty or more would seem ancient." That's how Lindy always felt. And now that she was in her thirties, fifteen seemed young.

"Yes. That's how I felt at the time. Iva May has been a real blessing around the town though."

"She is. She's been such a wonderful and supportive friend to me since I moved here." She paused, not wanting to pry. "Were you...planning to keep your baby?" Lindy asked gently, not sure she was overstepping, but Beverly was the one who brought the subject up.

"I guess I was. I was too young and dumb to really make a good decision, and embarrassed, and ashamed. Forty years ago, it wasn't quite the same as it is now."

"I know."

"But abortion was legal, and I considered it. Over the years, I've felt my baby dying was because God knew I'd consider doing that anyway. In fact, I would have if there had been a place nearby or I could have gotten one. But I would have had to travel to Chicago."

"I see."

"It was for the best anyway." Beverly sighed. "I wouldn't have been able to do what I did in the business world, to make money and donate to good causes, like the hospital that we have in Blueberry Beach. God had a plan for my life, it was just not what I thought."

"You were able to help a lot of people. There are people being helped at the hospital right now as we speak, because of the baby you lost forty years ago."

"That's right. I've reminded myself of that a good bit this morning already." She sighed and turned her cup. Again. Before folding her hands and looking up. "Life holds surprises. That's for sure. I wish you all the success in the world with your ice-cream store."

"Thanks, Beverly."

Beverly pushed back, picking up her undrunk coffee. "If you don't mind, I'm going to go take a little walk. I'll be back for the opening."

"Thanks. I don't mind at all, of course."

Iva May eventually came over and chatted a bit, talking about Anitra and how her son Jordan was doing, until it was time for Lindy to leave.

All the other shops on the street turned their signs over to CLOSED or locked their doors just for a little bit at ten o'clock, and all the owners showed up in her shop.

She felt supported and loved and included in their group, which was tight-knit and sweet.

Adam walked in as soon as she unlocked the door, and she felt guilty because he should have been in earlier and not waited outside like a regular customer.

She didn't have time to chat with him. It was early, but tourists had lined up outside the door, and Lindy was busy from the time she opened until closing.

Sierra was there for a while, then asked if she could go home if her dad would take her, around three o'clock.

Adam had stayed all that time, helping if he could, sitting out of the way if not.

Lindy, who was torn by happiness and a little bit of a bittersweet feeling, nodded.

It was so unusual to have help, to have a husband or maybe a father acting like a father, that she could hardly form words and was glad she could get away with nodding her head.

Things slowed down by seven thirty, and the store was empty by ten 'til eight when the bell rang, and Lindy looked up from where she was wiping up a little bit of spilled ice cream on the floor beside the cooler.

She stood, not recognizing the woman who walked in.

She had black circles around her eyes and seemed painfully thin, wearing a tunic dress, although the way she moved, just for a second, Lindy thought she might have seen a little bit of a bump of her stomach outlined under the dress before the woman shifted and the outline disappeared.

Maybe Lindy was just imagining things, thinking about babies and Beverly, and the woman, looking tired, with a deep sadness and maybe something else in her eyes, stepped up to the counter.

"I'm Anitra. I own the diner. I understand you've been helping a little over there."

"Oh my goodness. Anitra! Everyone talks about you. I'm so happy to finally meet you." Lindy wiped her hand off and held it over the counter. Anitra smiled and shook it.

"I was happy to see your ice-cream shop open." Her eyes fell for a little bit, and then she said, "My son, Jordan, loves birthday cake ice cream." She stepped back and looked down at the tubs of ice cream through the case glass. "Do you happen to have any?"

"I sure do. Would you like it in a bowl or cone?"

"A bowl, please."

Lindy dished the ice cream out, wondering if she dared to ask how Jordan was, then she decided she might as well. It wasn't like Anitra was trying to keep his sickness, or even his dying, a secret. She straightened, closing the glass and putting the scooper in the water.

"How is Jordan?" she asked as she picked up the bowl.

Anitra bit her lip but didn't hesitate to answer. "He's fading. I'm just so thankful that he's not in pain. He's not scared. He talks about playing baseball in heaven, and even though it makes my heart want to cry, it makes me smile to know that he's looking forward to the next step."

Oh boy. Lindy hadn't expected the words she said to bring such quick tears to her eyes. She blinked back.

"Here you go." She handed the ice cream over.

But Anitra was fumbling with her wallet. "How much?"

"No. Everybody got a free ice cream today. One. You can have one too if you'd like. Jordan doesn't have to be here to get his."

"No thank you. I'll...actually, maybe I will. Something with chocolate in it. Oh wait. No." She acted like the idea of chocolate made her stomach turn. Lindy thought again of the little bump that she thought she saw. "May I please just have plain vanilla? In a bowl. I'll carry them both over and eat mine with Jordan if he's up."

"Of course."

Lindy went back and dished out a bowl of vanilla, thinking about how hard it must be to know that your child is dying and have to watch it.

She couldn't imagine losing Sierra. It would be like having someone stick their hand into her chest and rip her heart out.

But one never knew. One never knew.

She was thinking about that as she handed the bowl of vanilla over.

"Are you sure I don't owe you anything?"

"No. Nothing." She wanted to give her a message to take to Jordan. Something she could tell her son about the ice-cream lady, but she couldn't think of anything that a little boy might want to hear from an adult that he'd never met. "Tell Jordan I hope he enjoys it."

"I will. You're very kind. Thank you."

"It was good to see you. Take care."

Anitra gave her a sad, tired small smile before she turned and walked out.

All Lindy knew about her was that her husband had been a huge jerk and had left after cheating on her multiple times. He hadn't been back to see his son since the cancer had come out of remission the second time. From what she understood, he hadn't been much help the first time either.

If Sierra had been sick... Adam had been busy with his job, but she was sure if Sierra had been sick, he would have done everything he could for her. He loved his daughter. There was no doubt.

And he'd been faithful. There had never been a whisper of anything regarding an affair. He'd always been very proper, very careful to be appropriate in every situation.

She had never had any doubts about his integrity, or his faithfulness, or his devotion to his family, even if it was misplaced with working long hours to provide for them.

No more customers came in for the night, and she closed, turning the lights off and locking the door with a sense of accomplishment.

She felt blessed.

She was healthy. Her daughter was healthy. And even if she lost the shop, if it wasn't a huge success, if she ended up not being a very good shop owner, she wasn't losing everything.

And she had Adam to fall back on. He might have neglected her. He might not have treated her well, but he would never let her be destitute. She knew he would work himself into the ground before he'd let her go hungry or without shelter.

Guilt clawed up the back of her throat. It threatened to choke her.

How in the world could she justify what she had been holding against him, the way she had, when he came humbly, contrite, seeking her forgiveness, apologizing? How could she not have accepted his apology immediately?

She kept thinking she acted like she knew she was guaranteed tomorrow.

She wasn't. Neither was he. Neither was Sierra.

They could be together as a family in half an hour. Instead, she was closing up and going home alone. While her husband slept in a tent in the yard.

That was sad.

She drove home, thinking about everything that seeing Anitra had started her thinking and what talking to her—and Beverly earlier in the day—had brought to mind.

She needed to make some changes. She needed to do some apologizing. She needed to get over herself and stop thinking that the world revolved around her and her pain and that not feeling pain again was the most important thing in the world.

How ridiculously stupid she'd been.

Maybe...maybe they should still take it slow. Maybe they needed to build a relationship, and that took time and effort on both their parts, but it was not right for her to dictate all the terms. It needed to be up to both of them.

Her husband shouldn't need to come crawling on his hands and knees groveling at her feet to "win" her affections. That was ridiculous, and for insisting on it, she really deserved to have him treat her just as standoffishly as she had treated him.

She had a feeling that he wouldn't.

But she knew she was going to find out. Tonight.

# Chapter 23

LINDY HAD JUST MADE the decision on the way home to ask Adam to move back in, when her phone rang.

Answering on the hands-free, she cringed when she saw it was her mom.

"Hello?"

"Lindy. I just wanted to let you know that we are on our way to your house. We're only an hour away, and I wasn't going to stop in tonight... But... The hotel that we normally stay at is booked solid. Apparently there's some kind of convention in town, and every hotel is sold out. I'm sorry to impose," she said, not sounding sorry at all, but like it was her right, "but would it be okay for your father and I to come and sleep on your loveseat?"

Lindy had to laugh. Although she tried to do it quietly so her mother wouldn't hear.

Her mother had absolutely zero intention of sleeping on her loveseat.

She wanted Lindy to say exactly what she was about to.

"You can have my bed mom. I'm on my way home. I'll change the sheets now."

"Thank you so much darling."

Then Lindy had a thought. One that made her mouth drop. The tent was in the yard and that's where Adam would be sleeping.

Oh, goodness, if her parents saw that her mom, at least, would be all over it. Wow.

But where was everyone was going to stay? She supposed...Sierra would give up her room, of course, but she just had a single bed.

"Lindy? Did you hear me? I said we can only stay one night. We're on our way to see your sister in Minneapolis. Her children are in an end of the school year program, and we're going out to see it."

"Oh. Okay. That's fabulous."

"You don't sound like you think it's fabulous."

"I'm sorry mom I was thinking. My shop opened today. First day. I don't open until dinnertime tomorrow, but I won't be able to come home after church. I'm opening as soon as the service is over."

"Oh. I see. Already your business is coming between you and the very limited amount of time you have to spend with your parents. That's fine. Maybe we can spend some time with Sierra and Adam."

Her mother probably didn't realize just how guilty those words made her feel. "Oh. That's another thing. Since there's really not a lot of room in our house, Adam and I might just go ahead and one or both of us will sleep in a tent outside."

Okay, she was kind of making it seem like the tent wasn't set up. She felt like maybe she was lying. It made her feel guilty.

"Actually, the tent is already set up, so someone might as well stay out there tonight."

"Why do you have a tent set up in your yard?"

"Mom. Don't you know everyone thinks tents are fun? And it's good to have family time together."

Okay that was a total non-answer.

She needed to think of something and fast to change the subject.

"So are you going to be stopping on your way back through?" she tried to make it sound like she wanted her to. She did love her parents, but her mom had a way of making her feel guilty about her shortcomings, and the fact that her husband was not sleeping in their house would be viewed as a major shortcoming.

"We might. We're staying a week out there. We can let you know. There's no rush to get back."

"Okay. That sounds fine. Just let me know. And we'll maybe keep the tent up."

"All right honey. Your dad's asking me to check the GPS again. I better go. We'll be there in about an hour."

"That's fine mom. We'll see you then."

They hung up just as she was pulling into their lane.

Oh, boy. She sighed, not liking that she felt like she had to hide something from her parents.

Adam would go along with it. She was sure he would, she just...She'd been intending to invite him to stay in the house, thinking she would sleep on the loveseat.

But...Maybe this was for the best.

She pulled in and could see through the picture window that Adam and Sierra were sitting at the puzzle table putting the puzzle together.

She sat in her car for just a minute, looking at that picture. For so many years she had done everything alone, and it was so nice, so very nice, to see him sitting with his daughter just spending time with her.

She almost wished she were there.

But, she felt like it was good for him to have time with just Sierra.

Plus, she planned to have Naomi and Lexi help in the store. There were evenings when they would all be home, and she had to admit, she couldn't wait. She wanted to be a family.

She wanted to enjoy the last few years that Sierra had left with them.

Just thinking about Jordan and Anitra, and the small amount of time that they'd had together, made her even more eager to appreciate the family that she had.

She walked in, tired, happy, and apprehensive.

Knowing she needed to talk to Adam about her parents coming, preferably without Sierra hearing, she tried to think of how she could do that.

"Hey guys. Wow, you have that almost all together."

"The pieces are going in really fast tonight for some reason," Sierra said. "Normally when I do a puzzle, I sit and stare at it, and get like one piece per hour."

"I think she's pretty good. She takes after her mom." Adam looked over the table at her. Her heart spun at his gaze. She tried to pretend it didn't.

"I see you guys left the sky for me," Lindy said as she walked over.

"We sure did. I'm not getting in trouble for putting it together." Adam raised his hands, like she would actually be upset or something.

"I just got off the phone with grandma and grandpa, and they are going to be here in an hour. They'll be here tonight, staying overnight, and will be going to church with us in the morning."

"They're really staying the night?" Sierra asked. "And they're staying *here*?"

"They are. Apparently the hotel they normally stay at has a convention or something and everything is all booked up."

"Wow. Where are we all going to stay?" Adam asked.

So much for talking to her husband about this by himself.

Lindy tried to look relaxed and cheerful.

"Well, I thought it would be fun if you and I stayed in the tent together?" She tried to make that sound like fun, but she was pretty sure it fell flat, since both of them knew they hadn't been staying anywhere together for months.

"That's fine with me," Adam said. Nothing he might be feeling showed on his face.

Maybe that was because Sierra was there, or maybe he really didn't care.

Except, there seemed to be a little extra...something in his tone. She wasn't sure what that something was, but it definitely made the inside of her stomach feel ticklish.

"I told them I would go ahead and change the sheets on our bed. So that's what I'm gonna do, and then I'm going to take a shower and maybe grab a few things to take out with me tonight."

Adam's eyes were dark, and they followed her as she moved over, straightening a picture that was already straight on the wall.

"That sounds good." Definitely his voice caused a riot in her chest.

It was so unfair that he could do that just with his tone of voice.

Rather than flutter about the room nervously, she forced herself to stand still and said, "Did you get your homework done, Sierra?"

"I did it last night, Mom."

"Perfect." She started walking away. "Well then, I'm gonna get going."

No one said anything as she walked away, annoyed with herself for being so obviously nervous.

Why?

It wasn't like she hadn't slept in a tent before. It wasn't like she hadn't slept with her husband before, either.

There should be no reason for any kind of extra emotion on her part.

But it was there. No doubt.

She'd gotten the sheets changed, and put the ones she'd taken off in the washer, and had showered and was just stepping into the hall when the door opened and her parents came in.

They spent a half an hour or more chatting, and thankfully, no one mentioned her leaving, and Adam selling the business or anything along those lines.

Apparently there had been a big traffic jam and a huge detour on their way in, and her parents spent a lot of time talking about that.

They were obviously tired though, and after Lindy had offered them food and they declined, her mother said, "If you don't mind, I'm exhausted. It'd been such a stressful day with that big backup, and all the detours that we had to do."

"There was no signal for our GPS, and we followed the wrong line of cars," her dad added, even though they'd already talked at length about all the trouble they'd had.

Lindy smiled. "I'm glad you guys made it safely, and you can certainly go to bed."

"I guess we'll head that way ourselves." Adam said, lifting his brows at her, as though asking if that was right.

She had no reason to stay up longer, and she nodded.

Her stomach twisted, and shook, and spun, and she didn't think it would ever stop.

What had she done?

# Chapter 24

ADAM HELD THE FLAP so Lindy could bend over and duck in. He considered turning on his phone so they had light, but she didn't turn hers on, and he decided not to, either.

They didn't say anything, and after a few minutes, there was rustling and movement coming from her direction. It would have been a lot more awkward with a light. He was glad he'd not turned it on.

The rustling beside him stopped, and he assumed she'd gotten changed.

It's been pretty chilly out in the tent, and normally he didn't wear pajamas to bed, but he'd had a pair of sweats and a T-shirt that he'd been using, just to stay warm.

He considered not wearing them. She wouldn't know he hadn't been doing what he always did.

But he didn't want her to feel threatened in any way, so he put his T-shirt on and changed into his sweats, fumbling to find them in the dark.

He didn't hear her moving and barely heard her breathing. He whispered in the darkness, "Are you okay?"

His heart pounded, and it felt like she had to be able to hear it filling up the space of the tent, which suddenly felt extremely tiny and not nearly big enough for two people. She didn't answer right away.

Finally, out of the dark she said, "I'm not sure where the sleeping bag is."

He reminded himself to go slow, it wouldn't be a great start to head butt her in the dark. He moved toward her, his hand out.

He touched something soft, and she jerked back.

"I'm looking for your hand," he said, just so she didn't think he was trying to do something weird.

Weird for that situation, not necessarily something he hadn't ever done before. It had been a while.

Her hand came out, waiting in the darkness, and brushed against his forearm, running down and taking hold of his fingers.

"I promise I didn't plan this," he said, goosebumps breaking out over his body.

"I know. I'm the one who talked to my parents and told them they could come. I don't know what I was thinking."

That made his heart sink and he wanted to sigh, but he knew she'd hear it and he didn't want her to know how her words affected him.

Obviously she wasn't happy with the situation, and maybe he shouldn't even be in the tent with her, but he was.

He used his other hand to find the sleeping bag, and he guided her hand toward it.

"Do you want to get in first? And then I'll get in after you're settled?

"I guess. I'm not sure on best practices for doubling up in a one-person sleeping bag."

"Me either."

This was one thing they hadn't done in their twenty year marriage. He figured it would be fun, would make new memories, and they'd know how to do it for next time. He wanted to make some goofy comment about it, but he kept his mouth shut. He didn't think a comment like that would go down very well, not right then, anyway.

She moved in the darkness, wrestling around, and he waited. It doesn't take long, until he heard her voice from the ground. "I'm in."

"Okay. I... I can't see anything so I'm gonna have to touch you."

"I know."

She didn't sound very happy about it.

He had taken his socks off. If he had been sleeping alone, he would have kept them on, especially as cold as it had been.

But, it wasn't exactly romantic for your spouse to put their socks on your leg.

Even though, plenty of times in their marriage it had happened to him. Lindy especially got cold feet at night. At least she used to.

He slid his legs in, very aware of his wife beside him, and hearing her breathing, smelling the scent that he'd missed and longed for, feeling soft skin and softer hair, and he wished, *he wished*, he could see her.

She was so beautiful. Maybe not classically beautiful where she would be featured on a magazine cover, or even win a local beauty contest. He didn't care. He'd never thought about her that way. She'd always been beautiful to him, because she loved him, and she was his.

He tried to think about that in present tense, because even though she still wore his ring, and she still had his name, he wasn't entirely sure she was still his. He wasn't entirely sure she still loved him, either.

Lindy was a woman of integrity and would not break a promise.

That alone made her beautiful to him.

He slipped the rest of the way in, and maybe he should have turned his back to her, but he didn't.

"I'm sorry, but I think it's kind of impossible for me to keep space between us."

"I know. It's okay. Do what you have to to fit in." Her words were softly whispered, but not in a tone of voice with a little sultry note that might say she was looking forward to having his arms around her, nor with a teasing note, that might say it's totally okay if he accidentally brushed something against something else, nor even a hesitant invitational note.

It was just softly said like she was saying it was supposed to rain tomorrow night and she hoped that wasn't a problem and do what you have to do about it.

Lovely. He was reduced to weather tones.

He had thought they were making progress, but this had probably set them back even more.

Still, he knew she had her back toward him, so he curled his body, fitting it to hers like they'd done so many nights before, and like she always loved. Her hips pressed against his and his legs curved with hers, and her feet rested on top of his. Maybe he was taking it a little far, but his arm slipped out and curled around her waist, tucking his hand under her rib like he always had, with his nose on her hair and his mouth by her ear.

He'd missed it. He wanted to say that out loud, wanted to tell her right there is where he wanted to be, and right there is how he wanted to sleep for the rest of his life. He longed, longed so fiercely he had to swallow because the words wanted to come out. His hand trembled and his breathing was unsteady. His heart raced, like it was trying to climb out of its cage and dance.

He swallowed and it felt like the sound echoed in the tent interior.

Maybe it was his imagination, but she seemed to have been holding herself stiff as he slid in beside her, but once he stopped moving, she settled, and he felt her relax against him.

Maybe she knew she couldn't hold herself stiff all night, or maybe it felt familiar to her as well.

He wasn't sure.

He did notice that her feet were bare, too.

That made him smile.

They were cold. He wondered if she took her socks off for the same reason he had.

That thought swirled around his head a little, giving him the first hope he'd had since they entered the tent together.

"Are you warm enough?" he whispered.

"Yes," she said.

Maybe he should have asked the next question first. "Are you comfortable? Am I squishing you?"

"I'm comfortable. You're not squishing."

If she wanted him to take his hand away from her ribs, she could have said so then. But she didn't. And the little bit of hope that had been floating around in his chest grew bigger, and he thought maybe this might have been a good thing after all.

Maybe she was remembering what she'd missed. What they'd missed.

He lay there for a couple of minutes, growing sleepy. He always fell asleep faster than she did. But an idea had been floating around in his head: he could take a risk. He could risk rejection.

Maybe he wasn't ready to know that there was no hope for their relationship, or that she wasn't interested in reconciling, but, maybe that was just the possibility of rejection that he needed to face.

"I missed this," he breathed into her hair.

She hummed.

He wasn't sure what that meant. But she hadn't said "I didn't." Which would have been worse.

"I missed you," he said, pushing a little, hoping to get a reaction out of her, hoping to figure out somehow that she missed this as much as he did and she was enjoying it as much as he was, and that she wanted this as much as he did.

He didn't want to spend another night away from her. Ever. For the rest of his life.

He remembered thinking that when they were first married, and he was ashamed at how far he'd gone away from what he wanted at the time. Away from what he'd promised her. Away from what she had expected when she said, "I do," and had allowed him to slip his ring on her finger.

But she didn't say anything, although he thought maybe she moved just a fraction of an inch, snuggling just that much tighter and closer to him. He squeezed a little with his arm, pressing her back to his front, and then, he moved slightly and kissed her head.

"Good night," he said, and maybe there was a little, or a lot, of longing in those words.

"Good night, Adam," she said.

At least she got his name right. He could find hope in anything, in any little thing.

He had to admit, he fell asleep that night with a smile on his face.

# Chapter 25

LINDY AWOKE EARLY. She always did. They were both morning people.

She had a feeling that Adam was awake behind her. She didn't hear the steady, even breathing that would indicate he was still sleeping.

He only snored when he lay on his back, and he was still curled up next to her, spooning her the way he knew she loved.

Of course, there weren't too many other ways for two people to sleep in a sleeping bag, although she supposed they both could have slept with their backs toward each other, but their feet still would have had to be entangled somewhat.

Whether or not he remembered about her cold feet, she wasn't sure, but they'd been warm all night, sitting on top of his.

She had taken a gamble with her socks, because cold feet would keep her up.

Normally, she was a pretty light sleeper, even more so when Adam wasn't around.

Which, for the last few years, had been almost every evening as she went to bed.

He said he tried to get into bed without waking her.

She had never been sleeping. She never slept until he came home.

She just quit waiting up for him. He hadn't seemed to care, and had seemed tired and preoccupied and never wanted to talk when he got home anyway.

Which was fine and understandable and it never made her mad exactly, just, made her feel like it was pointless for her to be awake and sitting up, if he was going to come home and grunt at her.

If she had said something to him, would it have changed anything?

Sometimes she wondered how he could have known if she didn't say, but when she did say a little bit, he always said, "I've got to get my business going." Or "I have to work this hard, so that we can be successful."

How could she argue with that?

Could she say, I don't want to be successful?

That wasn't true. She did, she really did want him to be successful.

She just wanted a husband as well. Wanted a father for her daughter. Wanted to have a family.

"You're awake," he said, his voice rumbling in her ear, raspy from a night of disuse and a little deeper as it always was in the morning.

"I am," she said, seeing no reason to deny it.

"Sleep well?"

"I did. You?"

"Best night's sleep I've had in...years."

She could say me too, but she didn't.

She just realized, she was going to have to get up and face him, with her morning breath and her bed head and her ratty jammies that were at least ten years old.

"Your feet stayed warm all night," he said, like he wanted to talk.

He always looked good in the morning, with the shadow of a beard on his cheeks, and his hair tussled, making him look like a little boy.

She'd always loved watching him in the morning.

It wasn't fair sometimes the way men looked better as they aged, looked better after a night's sleep, looked better after working all day, while women looked the best after they emerged after an hour and a half in the bathroom in the morning, and everything went downhill from there, and often times it didn't take too long.

She almost sighed then. She wasn't looking better as she aged, either. South seemed to be the general direction that all of her body parts were heading, taking her skin with them.

Wrinkles and age spots and gray hairs, all of which seem to be acceptable in a man, didn't work that way on a woman, and she had every single one of those, plus the middle-age spread hadn't exactly spared her.

Although, she still fit into the jammies that she'd worn when Sierra and she got matching ones...goodness, was it ten years ago?...for Christmas.

"They did stay warm. Thank you," she said, finally, figuring she ought to answer him.

She'd remembered shortly before he'd gone to sleep, he'd said he missed her.

She'd wanted to say she missed him – wanted to so bad – that she missed the snuggling and the feeling of safety and warmth and companionship and, just sharing her body heat with another human, the human that she was spending her life with, and, she had. She'd missed it. Badly.

But she'd missed it before she even left. She'd missed it for years.

Then she remembered what she'd thought about last night on the way home, before she'd gotten the call from her parents and her whole world had been turned upside down, and she thought that maybe it was a blip in the road from the Lord.

She could hardly hold Adam at arm's length, if she wanted to move closer.

Why was it always so hard to know where to start?

"You're probably not going to believe this, but last night on the way home from the candy shop, I had decided that I was going to ask you if you wanted to move back in the house."

She could feel that she surprised him. Just a little tightening of his muscles behind her, and he was quiet for a bit.

Outside the tent, the light was dim yet, signaling that it was early.

The first birds had started to chirp, and she listened until her husband said, "I believe you. I know you don't lie. Why?"

She had expected that. Of course he wanted to know why.

"I just realized how short life is. And, if I'm going to take a chance on someone, I might as well take a chance on my husband, right?"

That really didn't explain everything, but it probably explained enough. It was true. Seeing Anitra and thinking about Jordan had reminded her that life was short, and she needed to take the risk of exposing her heart, and possibly building something beautiful for the future.

Because who knew how much longer they'd have each other?

"I see. I guess I'm wondering what you mean by taking a chance on me? I mean, I know that you feel like I might go back and do what I did before, and I can promise you with all of my heart that I'm going to try as hard as I can to never ever let things go like that again. But, what does that look like...you taking a chance on me?"

Maybe he wanted to know what he could expect. Maybe he was allowing her to lead their relationship. He was standing back and telling her it was up to her.

That's what it seemed like anyway.

"Well...I was hoping we could take the tent down out of our yard."

He grunted, and she thought she felt his lips brush her head, and he seemed to bury his nose in her hair and breathe deeply.

She hardly felt anything but it was possible. She had just slept all night. Surely there wasn't anything that smelled good about her.

"I like that idea. Am I sleeping on the loveseat?" he asked, and there was an odd note in that question. It sent a little bit of a shiver down through her.

But she wasn't quite ready to go there.

"I thought I would."

"I can," he said, and she was pretty sure there was disappointment in that one.

"No. I will." She smiled a little. "At least, if I get tired of sleeping on the loveseat, that should move things along faster right?"

It was a gentle bit of teasing, and she wasn't sure he would find it funny. He might be frustrated with her.

But he chuckled against her, his chest rumbling just a bit, moving against her back, and she loved that.

"I guess. I like the logic anyway." He paused for just a second. "I don't suppose if I stuff the cushions with rocks, I could get away with it?"

"Now, why would you want to do that?" she asked, and there was some teasing in her tone then. He was a good man, fun, smart and everything she'd always wanted. And he had been making sure she knew she was important to him. She couldn't expect him to do all the giving. She had to start meeting him.

"Oh I don't know. I suppose if the loveseat is terribly uncomfortable, you might find somewhere else to sleep. I'll make sure I don't lock the bedroom door."

She heard his smile against her head.

"That was a hint you can tuck away somewhere," he added, still teasing, but she figured he was serious, too.

"Right. I'll remember that. Bedroom door is not locked."

She wouldn't have minded staying there, being held, for hours, but she needed to get up.

"My parents will be stirring soon, and they're gonna want coffee and breakfast and they're gonna want me to talk to them before church." She wished she didn't have to. She wished... There were so many things she wished.

He sighed and shifted. "I know. Do you want me to get out first?"

"Okay," she said, hoping that maybe he'd get out and leave the tent, so she didn't have to get up and let him see how terrible she looked in the morning.

She knew it wouldn't change his mind about anything, necessarily, because he'd seen her in the morning plenty of times before. But she didn't know if there was more reason for him to have quit paying attention to her than just getting busy in his business. Maybe he'd gotten tired of her. Maybe she wasn't appealing to him.

Maybe he was bored, or maybe something else had been wrong. She didn't know.

But she wasn't sure about him, and she didn't want to face him not at her best.

But there was no such luck, because he slipped out of the sleeping bag and sat in the corner behind her where he'd changed his clothes the night before in the dark.

It wasn't dark now.

And he just sat there, not making a sound.

She could feel his eyes on her, and she could picture him sitting, his knees with his forearms around them, and maybe one hand holding his wrist, and his eyes just parked on her.

She thought she knew the look that would be on his face, one of love, and affection, and just whatever it was that made him want to watch what she did.

He always seemed to love watching her.

Sometimes it made her self-conscious, but most of the time it made her feel beautiful. Like he always loved what he saw.

"Did you change your mind about getting out?" he asked.

"No." She almost said she was hoping he'd leave, but she didn't want him to think that she didn't want him.

They had been married long enough that he should know what the problem was.

She should have known he really did know.

He slid over and put a hand on her shoulder.

"You know you're beautiful to me, no matter what you think. And it doesn't matter to me whether your hair is short or long or whether you're bald. I really don't care."

"I know," she whispered, for some reason the back of her throat closed up and her eyes pricked.

"I don't care how tall you are. I don't care what the scale says. I don't care about whatever those things that you always worried about that were like dark things —"

"Age spots."

"I don't care about those. Wrinkles, whether your fingernails are painted or not. I don't care. I don't care about your warpaint, whether it's on or off, and I don't care whether your clothes are in style. I wouldn't know anyway."

"I know." She was able to get the words out, but her voice wasn't quite right. It was tight and a little squeaky.

"Don't you even," he said, and he sounded scared.

She laughed a little, trying to swallow back the tears that wanted to come. He hated it when she cried.

"I'm not," she said, but she kind of was. Because one tear had leaked out, rolling down her temple, and dripping into her hair.

"It sounds like you are. That wasn't the reaction I was going for."

"I know." She knew he wasn't. She knew he was trying to make her happy. And that's kind of what he did, but sometimes —

"I know. You're gonna say, sometimes you cry when you're happy. I don't believe it."

"I think someone said last night, 'Lindy, you never lie.'"

"Someone did say that. And...that's true. That, I *do* care about. A lot. Your character means a lot to me. That's what makes you beautiful to me."

The words made her throat tighten again. He had to stop.

She had to go to church, and before that she had to face her parents.

"I care that you love your family. I care that you have character, and integrity, and you do what you say you're going to do, and you do it as well as you can. You put your whole heart and soul into everything and you make it the very best. It might not be perfect. I don't care about perfection. I care about your attitude and your actions and the smile that you always have, and the way you determine that you're not going to be that angry person, and you're not going to be grumpy and miserable. I love that when people are mean to you, you're nice back. No one does that. It makes you special and unique and I love it. I don't even get it. But I notice."

She laughed. "I just never think they do it on purpose. I don't think people usually do."

"See? You always give people the benefit of the doubt. Do you know how rare that is?"

"You do it too."

"If I do, I learned it from you."

She rolled over on her back, wiping the tear track from the side of her eye.

"Thank you. I already knew you thought all of those things, but I appreciate you saying them. I know that's the way you are, truly. You're not just saying it. Because you've lived it."

He nodded, his lips turning up a little as he searched her face, seeming to make sure that she really was okay. That was another thing that proved he truly cared about her.

She could believe with her whole heart that the true reason he was trying to make his business as successful as possible, was not just because he wanted a successful business, but because he wanted to take care of his family, because he wanted her to be proud of him.

"You do know, I admire what you've done," she said, figuring that she had decided she needed to meet him halfway, at least. She didn't want him putting more into their marriage than she did.

Wouldn't it be better to have a competition as to who could do more for the other, rather than to see who could get more done for them?

"What do you mean?" His eyes had narrowed, like he was trying to figure out what she could possibly admire him for.

"Well, before that, I just want to say," her eyes roved over him. His T-shirt was old and thin, so were his sweats, but somehow he wore them with a masculine casualness that stirred her heart, and made her proud he was hers. "You look good first thing in the morning. I like this." Her hand reached out and she touched his cheek, rubbing a little on the stubble.

His hand came up, covered hers, and he moved her palm to his mouth and kissed it.

"I like this."

"That's my hand, you doofus."

"I see it. I like it." He kissed it again.

She laughed, but she didn't take her hand away, and he moved, his fingers linking with hers, as he pulled her hand higher and kissed her wrist.

She needed to get out, but she wanted to close her eyes, because it was so gentle and heartfelt, and it was more romantic than a million movie screen kisses.

"Are you ever gonna tell me what you admire about me? Or was that it?

"You're making me forget what I was going to say."

"I think you're just saying that. I think you're shallow. I think you care what I look like, that I have the movie star stubble, and the tousled hair, and I wear the right clothes. You want to see my six pack abs?"

She did laugh at that, because she knew there were no sixpack abs. But she also knew he wasn't the slightest bit self-conscious, and unlike her, he could lift his shirt and laugh at his flaws.

"I admire that you were so serious about wanting your family back that you sold your business and our house and you moved into a tent in our yard. If that doesn't say you're serious, I have no idea what does."

"Well, I want to tell you, maybe I shouldn't, but I don't think you should give in too easily, because I have a whole lot of other things planned. A whole big long list of things that I'm gonna do to win my wife back. So you better just keep giving me the stiff arm."

"Could I...stop giving you the stiff arm, and still maybe get some of those things?" she asked, and tilted her head, knowing she didn't look cute but batting her eyes anyway.

"Woman, you bat those eyes at me, and I might forget that your parents are in our house, waiting on us." His eyes got a little wicked. "They might wonder what's taking us so long when we don't show up for another hour or so."

She knew exactly what he was saying, and there was a large part of her that thought that it might be worth her mother's wrath to spend that hour with her husband.

"I can tell you're considering that. I kind of feel like I could sweeten the pot a little bit and talk you into it."

"Sweeten the pot?"

"But I'd better not, because I really don't like it when your mother's mad at me."

"She never gets mad at you. It's always me. You're definitely not going to get in trouble, but I'm going to get a lecture, except she's leaving today, so maybe I'll get a lecture tomorrow, or at least it won't be until this afternoon when she's in the car."

"How about I get up right now and save you from the lecture?"

"She likes your coffee better than she likes mine anyway."

"That's true. Your mother is kind of partial to me. I'm going to go take care of her. You can thank me later."

He gave her wrist another kiss, soft and gentle, which gave her goosebumps, and made her think again about not caring about whether or not her parents were upset.

He leaned forward, and she almost closed her eyes, thinking she was getting a good morning kiss for the first time in a long time, but his lips touched her forehead, and he said, "I love you Lindy. You know I never stopped."

He sat back though, and didn't really give her a chance to answer, grabbing his clothes and ducking out of the tent while she still had a dreamy smile on her face.

She watched him go. Then he disappeared as he zipped the flap closed, and she was alone.

# Chapter 26

SUNDAY EVENING, LINDY wiped the last counter off and straightened the bottles of ice cream toppings, the last chore before closing.

Her parents had gotten off alright. Adam had kept her mother happy, and he'd also kept his arm around Lindy though church. She'd basked in the feeling of her husband beside her and the sermon wasn't nearly long enough. Not nearly.

She'd gone to open the candy store after that, while Adam and Sierra had lunch with her parents at the diner.

Adam had come in with Sierra after her parents left. He'd mentioned Dr. Chambers had been at the diner and he'd seemed preoccupied.

After seeing Anitra for the first time, something that had bothered Lindy had spun through her brain at odd times. She couldn't shake the idea that there was something...something about Dr. Chambers and...Anitra.

If there was, that would explain the odd situation where a highly respected oncologist was working in the kitchen of a small, beach town diner.

Lindy loved a good mystery, but she had enough of her own problems and didn't need to borrow anyone else's. So she tried to let it go.

When Adam walked in, she forgot all about Anitra and Dr. Chambers.

Her heart jumped and pounded and she clutched her rag tighter to keep her hands from shaking.

173

"Hey," he said, and his voice gave her shivers, like they were twenty years younger and had never been married.

"Did you want some ice cream?" she asked, feeling like it was a dumb question, but not knowing what else to say. Her brain just wouldn't work.

"Looks like you have everything closed up," he said, walking over and standing on the other side of the glass cooler.

"I do. But I would get something out for you if you'd like."

"I'm fine. I just knew you would be closing up and didn't know if you'd like to take a walk on the beach." He seemed to hesitate. "Sierra and her band are practicing there. It's not like a real performance, but it should be good."

"I remember. A dress rehearsal." She wrung the rag out and glanced over everything, feeling a bit of pride along with the zaps of nerves.

"You have everything looking good in here," Adam said, changing the subject and seeming to read her mind.

"Thanks." She turned to look at him. "I'd love to take a walk." It was so true. She wanted to be with him.

His smile turned up both sides of his mouth and lit his eyes.

It made her heart warm and filled her chest to make him happy.

They walked out the door together and she locked it behind them. She'd barely pocketed the key, when he took her hand.

It felt perfect and right and she smiled.

Neither of them said anything as they walked down the sidewalk, the strains of the band carrying on the cool evening air.

"It's kinda neat to get to go watch our daughter play outside of a school setting." There was no mistaking the pride in Adam's voice as they walked out on the boardwalk and joined the back of the small crowd that had gathered around.

"It is," Lindy agreed. "It's nice to do it with you."

He flinched, just a small jerk, but it hurt her heart.

"I'm sorry. I didn't mean that as a hit. I meant it as a compliment – that I enjoy spending time with you."

"I know." He didn't need to elaborate. She knew what her words, unintentionally, had done.

Someone beside them jostled them, and Adam pulled her in front of him, wrapping his arms around her waist and dropping his head beside hers, his mouth at her ear.

"Being with you makes everything more fun. I'm sorry I spent so much time away from you."

"You don't have to keep apologizing. I believe you." Her head dropped back on his shoulder and she lifted her eyes, looking at the stars, a bit of sadness in her tone.

"But?" he asked, maybe responding to the sadness.

They couldn't move past this if she wasn't forthright. Hiding things and not talking about them wasn't going to help them heal.

"I guess I wondered if there was more than work that took you away."

He flinched again against her back and she regretted that her words caused him pain. But it had been a fear.

"That's part of the reason I didn't want you to see me this morning. I'm ugly in the morning."

"I told you I don't care."

"I know. But I thought maybe you just got tired of me, or wanted a new challenge or...I wasn't accusing you of having someone else, just that I wasn't appealing anymore."

"No!" His word came out low and fierce. "Never. It was always about building the business and making it successful. Never any lack on your part." He let out something between a sigh and a groan. "I hate that you think that, but I can understand why you might have. I stopped acting like you were important to me. Stopped doing the things that made you feel like I loved you. Man, you have no idea how sorry I am about that. How much I wish I could make it up to you."

His words had helped. She pretty much knew it was how he felt. "I needed to hear it."

"I'll tell you every day, two or three or more times, if you need me to."

"You've been showing me. That's better."

He smiled against her ear.

"I...I don't want you to do all the giving, though." It's what she'd been thinking and she wanted him to know it. He had to know she was serious about him, too, for this to work.

"Lindy. You stayed with me for twenty years. Fifteen of those where you were neglected and basically a single mom who did a man's laundry. You don't need to show me anything."

"I left."

"And that hurt."

"You haven't wondered about me at all? About how I feel?" His hands tightened around her and she knew her hunch had been right.

"I have. Of course I have. But if our relationship is a mess, it's not your fault. I don't want you to have to pay anything."

"But a relationship is two people."

"You're too generous. Too good for me."

The song ended and the crowd of people who had gathered clapped together. Lindy clapped with them, but Adam didn't move his arms from around her, didn't move his body from behind hers.

She shook her head. "I'm not. I'm not the slightest bit good. Please don't give me more credit than I deserve." She'd deserted her husband with no intention of going back. "If it weren't for you, we'd be separated. You're the one that has made tonight possible." She meant, not only them together, but as Sierra looked over the crowd and saw both her mom and her dad, her smile brightened and her posture straightened.

"This is the way it should have been all along."

She was sure Adam saw Sierra too, and he meant her as much as he meant them together.

They were quiet for a bit as the band moved into a new song and the crowd shifted – some leaving, some staying.

"If it's okay with you, I'll ride into work with you on Tuesday. I have your car scheduled to get new tires and the oil changed. I'll have it back long before closing." He paused. "There is a little life left in your tires, but the way it rains out here in the spring, I don't want anything to happen to you."

She closed her eyes and swallowed before taking a breath. "Thank you. Thank you so much." This is what she'd missed. Someone who loved her so much he took the time to make sure she was safe and cared for.

They stayed for a while, listening to their daughter, snuggled together, and they never did take that walk on the beach.

# Chapter 27

ADAM SPENT THE WEEK going into the surf shop in the morning after helping at the diner with Lindy. When he got off at the surf shop, he spent the rest of the day in the candy store with Lindy.

Even if it wasn't busy...especially if it wasn't busy. He tried to tease her and joke some, but also talk about more serious things too – the future of the candy shop, Sierra's summer plans and, finally, on Thursday afternoon when Naomi and Lexi took over the counter for a couple hours, he brought up their future.

They'd grabbed sandwiches at the diner and had found a place on the beach to sit and eat them. He'd pulled their water bottles out of his back pocket and she'd opened the paper bag with their food.

"I think I could live here forever," he said, by way of introduction to the topic he really wanted settled, but didn't want to push about.

"Me too," Lindy said with a dreamy smile that he'd seen over and over again since he'd come to Michigan.

"I think I'd like to travel some, too." He took the sandwich she handed him and said a short prayer.

As she unwrapped hers, she said, "I wouldn't mind. I suppose Sierra will soon be off doing her own life and it will just be us."

That's what he was hoping. His neck pricked and his stomach tightened. "Does that mean that I'm forgiven?"

Her brows puckered and she tilted her head at him. "I already said you were. I thought we'd settled that?"

His eyes met hers. "Have we?"

"I have." She set her sandwich down and picked up her bottle of water, taking a drink. "I really want you to stop feeling like you have to keep asking. In fact. I insist on it." She pursed her lips together like she was thinking, and then she said, "I also want you to take your tent down tonight. There's no need for it to stay up."

He nodded. "Seems like you're getting kinda bossy all of the sudden."

"Because I'm insisting this is not going to be all about me."

"I guess I could say 'game on,' because I'm not done making it all about you."

She lifted a brow in challenge. Then she smiled, a slow, curving smile that lit up her face and made his breath hitch. "This is the kind of competition I like."

"Me too."

"I want to put the past behind us. It can't be something that's constantly pushing into the rest of our lives. It's over. It's done. Let's let it go."

He nodded. They'd already been sitting side by side, but she leaned in to him, and, while there weren't many things that came between him and his hamburger, Lindy was one of the few people who could make him completely forget about his food.

He put an arm around her and drew her to him. He'd intended for her to lean her head on his shoulder as they sat and watched the lake, but rather than putting her head down, she lifted it, her eyes on his as she leaned closer.

Still, it surprised him when her lips touched his. Maybe he gasped a little. He definitely lost his balance, and they ended up lying on the sand, her body over his, her hands in his hair and on his shoulders and him equal parts wanting to enjoy his wife in his arms and wishing they weren't on a public beach.

Regardless, it was a long time before she lifted her head.

He couldn't quite drag his eyes open, but he was able to smile, at least.

"So, you agree with me?" Lindy asked, sounding as breathless as he felt.

"Yes," he said. "Whatever it is, yes."

She laughed and his chest clinched, then expanded, bigger than he'd ever thought it could. She settled down with her head propped on his chest and her body next to his.

"Come back in the house, Adam. Please?" she said.

He propped his other hand under his head so he could see her better. "You didn't have to add that 'please,'" he said. "It's what I want. I just don't want you to think that having you doesn't mean anything to me. Because it does – it means everything."

"As long as we're in a competition as to who can do more for the other, I don't think we're going to have to worry about anything."

They stayed on the beach for a while, finally going back to help the girls through the evening rush.

Sierra had come in after practicing with the quartet she'd help start, and the three of them closed up an hour or so after Naomi and Lexi left.

As they drove home together they talked about the candy store and music and summer plans, and then Sierra said, "Dad, did you tell mom about the black eyed susans you special ordered for our flower beds?"

Adam felt Lindy's eyes on him before he took the turn to their house and looked over at her.

"Adam?" she said, and her voice sounded breathless and excited and disbelieving all wrapped in one.

He lifted a shoulder, but kept his eyes on her face. She remembered. He was sure of it.

"I can't believe you remembered."

He smiled. He wanted to say, "Of course," but it wouldn't be accurate. There was nothing of his past actions that would say that he should have remembered her grandmother's house when they'd been dating and the patch of black-eyed Susans that Lindy had loved and where they'd shared their first kiss.

"I remember how beautiful you looked next to them and how much you loved them. How sad you were when your grandmother passed away and your parents sold the house." He looked at the house as he pulled to a stop. "I also remember you'd wanted me to go dig some up before closing, and I didn't have time. I've thought about that, and a million other things, since you left."

His eyes went back to her and he barely heard Sierra's door close as she got out of the car. "So many things I didn't do and could have. Should have."

Her eyes seemed to have filled with tears, although none had spilled over. She breathed deeply before she spoke. "I don't know if you've been doing all of this to make me fall in love with you all over again. For the record, I never "fell" out of love. I just lost my way for a bit. But, anyway, if that's what you wanted, it's worked, over and over and over. Thank you."

The tent was still in the yard, and Adam never did get it down that evening. But, he did move back into the house and back into the bedroom with the wife of his youth and the only woman he'd ever loved.

# Epilogue

ANITRA SAT BESIDE THE hospital bed in her apartment over the diner she owned in Blueberry Beach where her son Jordan lay dying.

She held his hand with one of hers. Her other hand lay over the small bump of her stomach where the sibling Jordan would never know lay snuggled and warm and safe.

She hadn't told the father, hadn't actually spoken with him again, and wasn't sure she was going to.

Jordan's dad had not come to see him one time since the cancer came back.

Obviously, she could live without a man. She could raise a child without a man. Hopefully she could bury a child without a man, because she was going to have to, and soon.

"Do you hear them, Mom?" Jordan asked in a raspy voice.

"The crowd in the baseball stadium?" she asked, knowing by now that's what he was probably talking about.

"Yes! They want me to go up to bat. They think I can hit a home-run." His eyes barely opened, but his thin lips were turned up in a smile.

"I know you can do it son." She stopped short of giving him permission. Whatever he saw in his head – if that's where it was – she didn't want to make the dream reality. Giving him permission to go, might mean he actually left. After all, he claimed it was Heaven and that he was going to get to play baseball with Jesus.

The thought sent all kinds of mixed emotions through Anitra. Happiness that her son wasn't afraid of dying, but sadness, of course, because she didn't want to see him go. Even though...she knew it was time.

Movement caught her eye and she looked out the window. The new shop owners across the street – Adam and Lindy Coates.

She'd met Lindy and had liked her immediately. She'd been compassionate without being nosey. Jordan and she had enjoyed their ice cream. Probably for the last time.

Swallowing against the pain in her throat, she watched as Adam put a key in the lock, then turned, grinning and saying something that made Lindy laugh.

Adam let go of the key and swooped his wife up, spinning her around and kissing her soundly. She kissed him back just as enthusiastically.

Anitra smiled, although it added to the painful ache already in her chest. A love like that was not something she'd ever be a part of.

She made bad choice after bad choice with men.

Her hand curved around her stomach. She wasn't even going to have the pretense of raising this child with a man. After all, she'd been married to Jordan's father but had done most of the work herself.

No point in getting married just to have a piece of paper that didn't mean anything. Not to her husband, anyway.

"Mom?"

Her thoughts came back to the room and to her son. "Yes?"

"I'm gonna be okay. There's gonna be a lot of little kids up there and Jesus is going to watch us until you get there. Okay?"

A little bit of red had colored her son's cheeks. He was almost too weak to move, but he somehow managed to look excited.

"Maybe I need to bring your bat and glove," she said, unsure what to say. Unwilling, still, to give permission.

"Nah. They have plenty and they're better than mine."

She swallowed. How could she deny her son? Wasn't it selfish to not let go? To not give her blessing?

"I hope you have a good time, Honey. You'll know I'll want to see what you've learned and how much better you've gotten when I get there."

"I'm gonna run again, Mom. I'm gonna be fast and it won't matter if I fall. I can slide into home base." A little bit of the boy he used to be came through in his little boy grin, despite the sickness that had eaten every last bit of fat from under his skin. "Don't worry about me, okay?"

"I won't, Honey. I'll come as fast as I can."

"No. Jesus said someone down here loves you. You need to marry him and raise my sister. She's gonna love baseball, too."

Anitra bit her lips. She supposed there was a fifty percent chance that the baby she was carrying was a girl. There was, however, a zero percent chance that she would get married again.

"Give her my bat and glove, okay, Mom?"

"I will."

Her words reassured him and, like he just couldn't hold his eyes open another second, they closed.

Assuring herself that his chest still rose and fell, Anitra checked the clock. Hospice would be here soon. Iva May after that. Maybe she'd take a walk on the beach. Not toward the pier. Definitely not. She didn't want to meet the father of her baby again and be tempted to lose her burdens in his tender, yet passionate, embrace. Once was one mistake too many. She had to be able to do this on her own. All of it.

On second thought, she'd call Iva May while hospice was here and let her know she didn't need to come tonight. No walking on the beach tonight. No losing her troubles in a man's gentle kiss.

She would do this herself. She most definitely didn't need, or want, a man.

THANKS SO MUCH FOR reading! If you'd like to read Anitra's story, you can get it HERE[1].

If you're interested in learning more about Jessie, she would love for you to sign up for her newsletter[2] – and get a free book not available anywhere else – or join her Reader Chat[3] on Facebook.

---

1. https://www.amazon.com/Tomorrows-Blessings-Blueberry-Beach-Novel-ebook/dp/ B08RW6CZVV/

2. https://dl.bookfunnel.com/97elto4gwl

3. https://www.facebook.com/groups/jessiegussman

Made in the USA
Monee, IL
25 August 2023

41627040R00105